228

MW01139340

This book is a work of fiction. The names, characters, places, and incidents are products of the writer's imagination or have been used fictitiously and are not to be construed as real. Any resemblance to persons, living or dead, actual events, locale or organizations is entirely coincidental.

Bullets aren't the only things flying on this mission...

When Texas Ranger Nash Sullivan finds himself in a hailstorm of gunfire during a bunker raid, he handles himself—and those around him—with his usual skill and sharp wit. It seems his charm worked its wonders too, because he's gone from a Ranger to a special ops unit captain overnight. His first assignment—find a man everyone's believed dead for the past decade. And he and his Ranger Ops team are going in.

Ten years ago, when Nevaeh Vincent's brother disappeared on a hiking expedition, her heart was torn out. Now, it's flayed open once more after her family is questioned again on the matter. She catches wind that the reason behind it is her brother's been spotted—and a special ops team is going undercover to find him. With that kind of hope, how could she ever stay away?

After Nash finds Nevaeh in a rough Mexican hostel asking all the questions that will get her killed, he has no choice but to take her along and protect her. Problem is her beautiful eyes are a distraction… and he can't quit thinking about latching onto those plump lips and showing her how to obey his every command. Nevaeh is here to find her brother. So why can't she ignore the sexy Ranger Ops captain? Could

these feelings be real or just aftershocks of her
adrenaline-filled journey?

Chapter One

"Good morning, sir."

"It's afternoon, Ranger Lieutenant."

Nash Sullivan had seen the sun rise two days and set two nights. He didn't know if he was even still on his feet let alone what numbers the hands on the clock pointed to.

He stood at attention before his superior officer, Colonel Robert Downs, Defense Coordinating Officer on the case Nash had just completed. The blinds were half drawn in the room, allowing the sunlight to slant across the table. It played with Nash's eyes, sending visions of the shadows made by chopper blades over the baked earth through his mind.

"Go on, Sullivan. Give your report."

"Sir, I am Ranger Lieutenant Nash Sullivan of Rangers Company A. My team consisted of nine other men sent to neutralize the threat along the Sabine River. Do you want me to name my team members, sir?"

"No, I know who they are. Just give your statement, Ranger Lieutenant." Nash's superior wasn't a man he knew well—only knew *of*. The stuff of legends, a decorated Texas Ranger who served a decade before his promotion to an advisor to the US military. And how he'd come to take interest in what was a relatively small threat in the US was a question mark in Nash's mind. After a grueling two-day battle, though, he may not be thinking straight.

Nash continued, "We arrived at O-four-hundred. It was still dark. I ordered my guys to split into teams of two and surround the building, which was a metal garage, sir. We didn't hear any noises and slipped in without detection."

As he spoke, the story came in spurts as he relived some of the moments before the words came to his mind. Basically, what he relayed to Downs was a clusterfuck. A raid that didn't stand a chance against the twenty-two terrorists holed up in that fucking garage—yet somehow Nash and his men had pulled out a Hail-Mary and done their jobs.

He didn't express how damn lucky they all were to walk away with their lives and only some minor cuts and scrapes among them—he only stated facts. That they had rooted out the guys in the garage, taken heavy fire, returned it and he himself had killed at least four of those bastards. His partner, Shaw Woodward, or Woody had taken down more. With his sharpshooter skills, the man was priceless as far as sidekicks went. If Nash was ever called upon for a duty like this again, he'd want Woody on his six.

When he finished speaking, Downs did not move or even twitch an eyebrow. He simply stared at Nash.

"That's all, sir."

"I see. Ranger Lieutenant Sullivan, have you ever been called on within Company A to handle a threat of his magnitude before?"

"Not quite like this, sir, but I've dealt with some shit in my days with the SWAT team."

The man didn't take offense to Nash cussin', which was a relief. He was too dead on his feet to guard his tongue, but Downs had led men before and knew their vocabulary consisted of the words fuck, hell, move and now.

Downs templed his fingers and contemplated Nash. He bore the scrutiny, prepared for any feedback on how he had led his team, good or bad. He'd made choices out there—some not so great—but none of his men were in body bags, so he wasn't going to apologize.

And if he did have issues with how Nash had handled things, well, he'd heard it before, that his temper took things too far and he needed to restrain himself. Hell, even his own brother said the same, and he'd gotten himself in a world of trouble nobody could help him out of.

Nash's shoulders ached. He hadn't sat down in hours and didn't know when he would again, at this rate. His mind was still laser-sharp, though. Nothing else mattered.

Just as he began to think Downs was just fucking with him, the man cleared his throat. He ran his hand through his high-and-tight haircut that was peppered with gray.

Nash waited.

"I don't often run across people I am impressed with, Sullivan."

"Sir."

"But I've seen Army Rangers fuck up missions like this, while you took nine men and got them into a position to take down those bastards. You realize the number of explosives we found on that property was enough to leave a big crater in the South."

"Yes, sir."

"From my standpoint, you are a bigger asset to the country than your role as a Texas Ranger allows you. And it just so happens that I have a job for you."

Nash's heart kicked up. "Whatever it is, sir, I hope I can get some sleep first."

He chuckled, eyeing him up. "I think a few hours can be arranged, but there's a unit forming right as we speak. If you're up for the challenge, I plan to send you and some of the men you fought with the past two days to Mexico."

Nash might have grinned if he had the energy. "I'd be honored, sir. Challenge accepted."

"Good." He stood and faced Nash. "Welcome to Operation Freedom Flag."

Nash straightened. "Operation Freedom Flag, the division of Homeland Security, sir?"

"The very one. You may have heard of a special ops unit operating in the South."

Knights Ops was known everywhere, though the team were like shadows, legends that nobody knew the real details of.

"Congratulations, Sullivan. You'll be leading Ranger Ops into Mexico. Do your country proud, Captain. Now go grab some rest. You deploy at O-six-hundred."

Nash reeled with all this information dumped into his tired mind. All he could do was thank Downs and take his leave. Once in the hallway, he stopped and stared at the wall for a moment.

Down the hall, a door opened and one of his guys walked out, looking similarly dazed.

Nash headed for him. "Linc."

Looking the worse for wear, with several abrasions down his face, where he'd obviously skidded on some rough ground, and sporting a crisscross of butterfly bandage strips above his left brow, Lincoln had likely never seen that kind of action as a Ranger investigating petty thefts.

He'd held his own, though, and Nash was damn proud to serve with him.

Linc lifted a hand and scratched at his head. "I don't rightly know what just happened in that debriefing."

Nash watched him closely. "Were you told to get some rest because you're hitting the ground running again in a few hours?"

He nodded. Suddenly, a big grin hit his face. "Do you think we're all going? Are we all part of Operation Freedom Flag now?"

Nash started to reply that he didn't know when Woody approached. Fatigue hadn't taken the cockiness out of Shaw's walk as he strutted toward them like he wore cowboy boots and a Stetson rather than tactical hard-soled boots and camo.

He shot them both a grin. "So... OFFSUS." The anagram stood for Operation Freedom Flag Southern US division, and Nash had never in a million years expected to become part of it.

Linc shook his head. "Hold up. Don't tell me they're calling Texas the South. It's the West."

Nash groaned. "You're not one of those guys who argues where we belong on the map, are ya? But yeah, you too, Woody?"

"Yep," Woody drawled.

Nash slapped him on the back, and Linc grabbed Woody's hand in a bro-grip. The trio stood there speaking quietly, when another door opened. A guy they'd just fought with emerged, slump-shouldered.

When he turned and walked the other direction, Nash watched him go.

"I don't think he's in," Linc said.

"He didn't handle that last shot well. Did you see him curled up in the corner like a bug?" Nash shifted his weight on his tired legs. "He's cut out to be a Texas Ranger, dealing with drugs, illegals and human trafficking. Now it seems like we're facing something altogether different." The motto of 'One Riot, One Ranger' didn't seem right in this case.

"What is it the Knight Ops say? Guts and glory one mission at a time." Woody's words fell over the three of them. They stood in silence for a moment, and Nash was finally sucking in the enormity of his sudden shift in career paths. When he'd watched the sun rise over the land, he'd been a Texas Ranger and damn proud of it.

Now he was a special ops force protecting his country. A captain.

"Damn, I must have charmed the hell out of Downs."

"Shit, you debriefed to Downs and impressed *him*? He's got brass balls, I hear." Linc raised his brows.

Woody just peered down at Nash's knees until he looked himself to see what was there.

"What is it?" Nash asked.

"Just checking if you wore a hole in those cammies after giving Downs all that head."

Nash burst out laughing and reached out to cuff his new buddy. Finally, three other teammates joined them in the hall, all appearing as stunned as Nash felt upon first hearing their new status.

Looking from face to face, Nash's chest swelled with what could only be pride. He stuck out his fist into the center of the circle. "Looks like we've got our six. Guts and glory—"

"One mission at a time," they finished with him.

* * * * *

"Evenin', Sully."

Nash nodded at the greeting as he walked through the Texas Rangers office. He wasn't certain who had learned of his shift in position, but he got several nods of hello as he made his way past them.

After Nash rapped on the door of Lieutenant Jack Lang's office, he didn't wait for a call to enter. He just pushed inside the small space and plunked into the chair that was practically molded to his ass because he spent so much time sitting here, shooting the shit with his mentor and friend.

Lang tugged the brim of his hat, a habit the man had since Nash had met him five years ago when he'd been transferred to Waco.

"Look what just walked through my door. Ranger Lieutenant Sullivan. Or should I call you captain now?"

Nash threw a look behind him at the closed door, but nobody had followed him. "Who all knows?"

8

"Just me." Lang sat back and hitched his boot over his knee, rocking lightly in his beat-up desk chair he claimed he spent too much time in rather than days out on the beat, but Nash knew his older bones and joints bothered him. After years as a Texas Ranger, the man was pretty worked over physically, and he had all the creases around his eyes to reveal the strain he'd spent decades under.

He wasn't sure what to expect from Lang.

"You might as well tell me what you think now and stop beating around the bush," Nash drawled. But he was nervous. This was a huge leap for his career, and after only one mission, he realized he'd only been priming himself all these years for it.

He was also nervous to hear what Lang thought. They worked closer than anybody in this office, and Nash was man enough to admit that the man who'd started off bossing him around—and telling him off about his temper—had become a good friend.

"What do I think?" Lang eyed him.

"Yeah."

"I think what matters is what you think."

Nash considered the question a moment. "It's a chance to use my skills outside of inspecting immigration papers and going on drug raids."

"You've done more than that with the Rangers, boy, and you know it."

"I've dabbled in a bit of everything, that's true." Hell, until being sent to the Sabine River and

9

neutralizing a threat that could have easily turned into a national day of remembrance, Nash had felt pretty damn confident he'd seen everything. He'd operated in a host of specialized units within the Texas Rangers, but the SWAT team, bomb squad and Ranger Reconnaissance Team hadn't shown him half of what he'd faced the past few days.

Lang grinned, which shot those creases around his eyes upward. "You proved the hell out of yourself, Nash. That's sayin' something."

Suspicion sneaked into Nash. "This was your doing." That old anger flared inside him.

Lang could always tell when Nash was about to go off, and he lifted a brow in challenge. At once, Nash pressed his fist to his lips, pushing down the emotion that had earned him a reprimand more than once.

"No, no. This was your doing." He shook his head and tugged his hat—an action that showed Nash he was telling the truth. "But Downs might have gotten a call through to me to ask my opinion on the matter of giving you that captain badge. All I did was flip open your file and read to him about your flawless commitment and wide range of skills."

Touched, Nash said, "Thank you, Lang."

"No need to thank me. You did it all, like I said. Now, tell me the details, or can't ya? It's probably all classified now, and we'll have to stick to shooting the breeze about horses and pretty girls."

Nash chuckled. His own pair of horses was boarded at Lang's place, and they rode the trails as often as possible together. But as far as pretty girls went, it was nothing but talk. Nash was too busy with long shifts, and Lang had buried two wives now and wasn't on the market for a third. Nash couldn't blame him.

"Not everything is classified. I can tell you that I'll be leading a fine team of men who proved they can work together on the fly."

Lang nodded again. "You need good men. You got a sharp-eye?"

"Couple. Besides myself." Nash grinned, because this was another point of teasing between them. Lang was always challenging him at the shooting range, and often they walked away at a draw with Lang always insisting on buying the beers even if he managed to best Nash.

"One's Shaw Woodward," Nash said.

"Damn, that's good luck, isn't it? The man's known for his ability to analyze situations on the fly."

"It helped a lot down at the Sabine. I look forward to working more with him." Nash glanced at his watch.

"Got someplace to be, Captain?"

Nash looked up with a crooked smile at the address. "Yeah, I gotta run. I just wanted to stop in here and see if you'd gotten up out of your chair yet today."

Lang rocked in it again. "Haven't felt the need yet."

With a chuckle, Nash stood and reached across the desk. His friend got to his feet without wincing at the arthritis in his knees and came around to take Nash's hand. When they gripped in a firm shake, Lang pulled him in.

"We're better friends than that, Nash." He clapped him on the back.

Nash pounded him in return, affection rising in his chest for the man he'd seen daily for so many years. That was about to change. "Every chance I get, I'll be in here bugging you. So keep that chair open, ya hear?" He pointed to the seat he'd vacated.

"Who knows when some young, cocky new Ranger will walk through those doors? Somebody's gotta try to fill those boots o' yours."

"Not fucking likely." Nash shot him a grin and then walked out of the office.

* * * * *

Nash climbed behind the wheel of the SUV and glanced in the rearview mirror at his four teammates taking up all the space in the back. At his side, Woody unwrapped a piece of gum and popped it in his mouth.

Nash sighed. His 'T's were crossed and his 'I's dotted. He'd made peace with Lang as well as his

12

family in the event that shit went south and he didn't come back.

Funny how as a Texas Ranger he'd always taken this for granted, though he'd faced dangers every day. Early on, he'd been taught that you couldn't count on the hours you stood on this earth.

He'd had a good buddy die during an assault, one by gunfire and even one in a gully-washer flash flood that had swept him under while he tried to rescue a woman and her son from a car in the rushing water.

That one still haunted Nash, because he was supposed to be on that call, and he'd always wondered if he had been present would his friend have survived.

He shook off the thought and started the engine. The SUV was as silent as a tomb, which led him to believe all of them were weighing their lives in their minds the way he was before heading off on their second mission as Ranger Ops.

He had to say something.

"Look. We've got a lot of work to do together, and we're just getting started. We need to know each other inside and out to form a solid team. What we did back there on the Sabine was our skills coming together, but we need to know what the other is about to think before he thinks it."

13

"Hell, this ain't the Knight Ops. They're all brothers. They were raised knowing what the other was about to think," Linc said from the back seat.

"No." He stared at his buddy in the rearview. "But we got a brotherhood. We're all Rangers. We had the same training, dealt with the same asshole bosses, and Texas people are the same across the counties."

"That's true," Woody said from the passenger seat.

Nash held out his hand for a piece of gum, and Woody gave him one. "We're gonna start this drive over the border with a kindergarten introduction. State your name, shoe size, all the names of your immediate family and whether or not you can handle your burritos so we can avoid them in the drive-thru."

That brought out the laughter. In the third row seat, two of the guys he knew less than the others shared a grin.

Nash slid the SUV into reverse and backed out. "Cavanagh, you kick off."

The muscled giant in the very back looked to be jammed shoulder-to-shoulder with his seat partner Jess, but it was only because they were both massive men.

"Wraggs, Cavanagh, shoe size fourteen."

"Damn, I knew you were big but fourteen?" Woody twisted in the seat to look back at him.

14

In the rearview, Nash caught the guy's smile. "Yeah, I buy my pants bigger too, to accommodate what I'm packing. Because yeah, it's true what they say about shoe size and dicks."

Jess elbowed him. "Man, you wish. I've seen you take a piss."

"You wanna compare, bro?" Cavanagh leaned back and reached for his fly.

"All dicks will remain tucked away, boys. This ain't no sausage party," Nash drawled.

The SUV boomed with laughter. When they settled a bit—it was *just* like a kindergarten class, or least high school—Cavanagh continued. "I served my country two tours in Iraq. Would have done more but I came back when my pops died and I had to support my mom so she didn't go homeless. She's my only remaining family. And yeah, I can out-eat all of ya when it comes to Mexican food. The hotter the better."

Jess shook his head. "You better not be lyin', Cav."

White teeth flashed. "Try me."

They moved to Jess. The Texan looked as if his cowboy hat was a bit too loose around his ears after he'd taken the time after the Sabine mission to shave his head. When he opened his mouth to speak, Cavanagh nudged him. "First, tell us why you shaved off your hair."

15

"Well, I'm known for those flowing locks, it's true, and the ladies love them." He doffed his hat and rubbed his sheared scalp. "But I figure I don't know what hole I'll be sleeping in next, and I hate bugs or lice. Can't tolerate 'em so I figured I'd get rid of anything legs could cling to."

"Your girlfriend cried, I bet." Nash made a right turn onto the interchange headed south to the border.

"Nah, she skipped out a week ago. Couldn't handle all this man." He rubbed his hands in circles over his broad chest, making everyone laugh. "Skipped out with a realtor. Only now I'm pretty sure it was the same guy who showed us our apartment. Huh." He dazed off a moment on that thought and then snapped back and recited the names of his mother and three brothers. Jess then told a tale about being so gassy after eating burritos that his momma made him sleep in the yard, he had the guys in stitches. Finally, he ended with crossing his boots. "And these, men, are my size twelves, which I am more than willing to shove up anyone's ass for crossin' me. They call it a Jess Monet enema, after me."

Cavanagh cuffed him in the ear, tilting Jess's hat. The smack talk that followed had them all bonding even more.

When they got to Lennon, he and Linc exchanged a look. The brothers were from opposite ends of the state and didn't work together, but Nash guessed the government had seen how well blood brothers

16

worked on a team like this with the Knights and paired them for the long haul.

"Reed, Lennon. Size eleven and a halfs. Got me a half size on my brother, but that figures because I'm much bigger when it comes to the man parts." Lennon's Texas drawl was deep and syrupy with a slow roll to his words.

Linc cocked his head at his brother. "In your fucking dreams, man."

Lennon went on. "This ugly fuck on my left is my twin brother Lincoln Hargrove Reed, and back at home I got a daddy who never had much time for me and a dog staying with a buddy."

"That buddy's sure got long, tan legs," Linc added.

"Wait, twin brother?" came the question from Jess.

"Yeah, we ain't identical, case you didn't notice," Lennon said. "I'm the good-lookin' one. Easy to remember."

"Never would have guessed at the twins part," Woody added.

"Because he's uglier," Lennon stated.

Linc rolled his eyes. "Get off my dick. And no, he can't handle his fucking Mexican. His eyes water like a little girl's the minute a jalapeno touches his tongue. I've seen him shit through a screen door at five paces after a good tamale too."

17

Woody laughed till his eyes watered, and Nash had to grip the wheel to hold it on the road for a minute. After they'd all gone through their introductions, which included three hell yeahs for the burritos, two size twelves and a ten and several brothers and a sister collectively.

With the ice broken, Nash felt he could speak on a different level to his men. Now that they'd let loose, they could get down to business.

"We're headed to Coahuila, men. There's a cartel there that keeps breaching the US border and distributing millions of dollars' worth of meth. It was the biggest dump we've seen in the past two years." The details he'd been given played in Nash's mind.

"How'd they get it into the country?" Linc asked.

"PA system."

"Come again?"

"They filled a truck with big speakers you use in concerts, and they were packed full of the shit. Took our guys two days before they discovered it, and by that time, the cartel was long gone. What I know is they're operating smooth, made a legit business down in Coahuila, and the guys who have gone in the past to shut them down can't find a damn thing. But that's ending here, Rangers."

The talk continued another hour as they crossed over the border. By the time they reached the capital city of Saltillo, all jaws were locked with determination and they knew the plan inside and out.

18

Nash rolled through an intersection, scanning the streets left and right, when he saw it.

He jerked in his seat.

"Shit," he muttered.

"What is it? Forgot to call your momma to tell her you won't be home for supper?" Woody ribbed him.

Nash gave a shake of his head, unable to joke at this time, not after he'd just spotted something that had his radar up and all his cylinders firing.

"Did you guys just see that man? The one in a black ball cap?" He swung his head to look at Woody.

"No, man. What about him?"

He blinked several times, but nothing would erase the image floating behind his eyes, a photo of a man that was plastered over every Rangers office in the state of Texas. A photo of a man who'd been missing for a decade and believed dead.

Nash took out his cell.

"He did forget to call his momma!" Woody and all the guys broke into laughter.

Nash dialed Downs. Realizing he wasn't laughing, the guys sobered and stared at him and each other like he'd lost his mind. When he got Downs on the phone, he spoke his thoughts aloud for the first time.

He wasn't fucking wrong about this.

"Sir, I need all the information you can gather on the Antonio Vincent missing person case."

19

Five heads jerked his way. Downs started firing off questions.

For the first time in his career, Nash felt he might have found his true calling and could actually do some good in this fucked-up world they all shared.

In his ear, Downs was telling him to focus on the mission and not to get sidetracked, but Nash couldn't let this one go.

With all the force backing his beliefs, he said, "I require all the information you have, sir, because I just saw Antonio Vincent, and he's alive."

Chapter Two

"Nevaeh, don't forget your lunch," her mother called from her spot on the front porch as she watered her flowers.

"I won't, Momma." She was running late as it was, and the last thing she had time for was making herself something to eat, but she couldn't afford to go out to lunch daily with the office ladies either. Besides, they didn't really enjoy her company, and she could do without theirs too. She much preferred to hide in her cubicle.

As Nevaeh grabbed her lunch bag and began to toss bottled water and fruit into it, she thought ahead to the long to-do list she was facing on a Monday morning, especially with the corporate meeting midweek. Of course she had tons of files to pull, and it was her most hated task.

"Nevaeh!"

"I'm packing it right now, Momma!" she called back.

"Nevaeh, come out here, please."

She stopped. Her mother's voice sounded strange, and the strain of the tone wheedled into the deepest recesses of her mind. Her stomach knotted.

Dropping what she was doing, she drifted to the front door where her mother stood on the other side of the screen with two men wearing suits.

Nevaeh's heart jumped into her throat and sat there, throbbing hard. The suits she recognized. Year after year of questioning, year after year of the authorities coming to gather more information that they'd already been told about her brother's disappearance. When Antonio had vanished, her family's life had been turned upside down and it would never be right again.

But they'd had a spell of peace—six years, to be exact—where nobody had come to ask any more questions and she, her mother and her father had cried most of their tears and begun to realize Antonio was never coming home, not even in the form of remains.

That old protective armor that Nevaeh had spent so long shrouding herself with steeled her spine as she opened the screen door.

Her mother's gaze swung her way, and she was already crying. "Oh, Momma." She reached for her mother's hands, worn thin from wringing them. They trembled in her grasp. "I'll speak to them." Send them away, more like. "Why don't you go on inside?"

"No. If they have found something this time…"

"Momma, you're already worked up. Let me speak to them alone, and I promise I'll sit and explain all that was said to you and Dad afterward." Her father had been wrecked by it all and could barely function enough to go to work part-time at the home building center. The entire family had been destroyed, but Nevaeh was strongest, and she'd handle it.

The two men continued to stare at them as she pushed her mother gently toward the door. She went, and the screen closed behind her. Nevaeh glanced back to ensure her mother was moving into the house, out of earshot, before turning back to the uniformed men.

Texas Rangers, this time. They seemed to be the most diligent over the years about Antonio's case, looking for any leads long after the state police filed the case as unsolvable.

She wrapped her lightweight blazer closer over her chest and greeted the men. "What can I do for you?"

"I'm Texas Ranger McCathrey and this is Ranger Michaels. We'd like to speak to you about your brother Antonio Vincent."

Just hearing his name always gave her a pang, but she was accustomed to the sting. She brushed it off and straightened her shoulders. "How can I help?"

He opened his mouth to speak, when a high, thin wail came from inside the house. The Ranger met Nevaeh's gaze.

"My mother," she said faintly. "The sooner you ask your questions, the better. She can't settle down until you leave."

"I'm sorry for your trouble, miss. I know how this must affect you all."

"Every damn day," she bit out with no less than the bitterness she felt at years of unrelieved pain, sometimes diluted by life but not often enough for any of them.

"Again, I apologize. We have some questions concerning your brother. If you can answer to the best of your knowledge."

She nodded.

"We know he visited Mexico at the time of his disappearance. A hiking trip?"

"Yes."

"Was he a regular hiker? Did he ever travel to hike in the United States or here in Texas?"

"Of course. He was always going out to the trails nearby and sometimes with friends to other parts of the country. Once in Colorado. What is this about?"

The Ranger continued without addressing her question. "And we have in our files that Antonio was skilled in technology. Mainly computers."

"Yes, he was always online. You confiscated his computer—is that in your files or did it go missing too?"

"We have the information noted here, yes. I wondered if you can tell me more about the computer skills. Was Antonio ever involved in online gaming?"

Inside the house, her mother's wail continued. She knew her father would be doing his best to quiet her, but it wouldn't be enough. Nothing was ever enough. Nevaeh wished these men had never come here. She could ask them to leave, refuse to answer questions, but what good would it do? In the end, her family needed closure, even if it was in the form of her brother's remains.

She brushed the chill bumps off her arms and said, "He was always online, obsessed with tech." Her mind lit on something. A spark flitted through her consciousness, long buried and only now resurrected by this specific question.

"Miss Vincent?" The Texas Ranger leaned in to peer at her.

She lifted her gaze to his. "I... remembered something."

The men exchanged a glance, and the one performing the questioning said, "Go on."

"One time I walked into Antonio's room without knocking. On his computer screen were long numbers after long numbers, rows of them. He didn't know I was standing there, and I didn't make a noise because I was his pesky kid sister and I knew he'd kick me out as soon as he heard my footsteps." She dashed her fingers through her long hair that her coworkers called mahogany and were forever saying they were going to get their hair stylists to match their color to.

"I'm listening," the Texas Ranger urged.

"Well, the memory isn't entirely clear, only that I was standing there not understanding what Antonio was up to. But he was typing fast, really focused on the task. And suddenly a warning popped onto the screen, flashing a word."

Her heart was pounding, and somewhere in the recesses of her mind, she registered what this could mean—that her brother might have been involved in something illegal. How could this have escaped her until now?

It was the pointed question about his involvement in technology, whereas in the past, everyone had solely focused on where he'd gone hiking.

"What was the word? Do you remember?"

Meeting the Texas Ranger's eyes, she nodded. "Restricted."

A fleeting interest washed through his eyes, and then he scribbled on his notepad. "And you have no idea what site he was on? What he was doing?"

She shook her head. "I only just recalled it. Because after the word flashed up, he moved and I ran down the hall before he could catch me in his room. I was just fifteen and still afraid of my big brother, especially since he was in college."

A moment of silence stretched, and her mother's wail had thankfully silenced.

Nevaeh narrowed her eyes. "What is this about? Why are you coming here again, after all these years? Have you reopened the case or something?"

"The case was never closed, miss. We were sent to gather more information."

"But why? Something must have spurred you to come back here?" Deep down, she had an inkling, a sixth sense. But she wasn't about to voice it, because she couldn't risk being wrong and dashing all hopes yet again.

"There has been a breakthrough to your brother's case, and we wished to speak to your family again. Are you certain your parents won't talk to us? Maybe they have other —"

"No," she said with force. The man stepped back a bit. She threaded her fingers in her hair again. "No. They cannot discuss this anymore. It's been a decade of being broken, and your coming here has already shattered what peace they might have found in the past few years."

"Again, I apologize."

"A breakthrough," she spoke up. "What sort of breakthrough?" Dammit, this was what she'd spent years building up a wall around herself for, so she wouldn't be disappointed again. She wasn't back to square one, yet she felt a chink taken out of that wall too.

"I'm not at liberty to give out that information, miss. But I'm certain someone will be visiting you if that changes. Is there anything more you can think to tell me?"

She shook her head, her mind already taking her leave of these men. It was running wild over the possibilities. If maybe they could follow a path to where he'd disappeared after checking into that Mexican hostel where he'd last been seen...

She turned for the house, and the Texas Rangers said goodbye before climbing back into their vehicle. Nevaeh didn't immediately enter the house, only stood at the screen door. Something—she didn't know what—made her press her nose to the screen like when she was little. Another memory surfaced, of her brother on the other side, pressing his nose to hers, both squashed on the metal fibers.

She jerked back, gulping down her emotions. This had to end—one way or another, she had to find closure, and not only for her parents. She too had been suffering for far too long.

With three weeks' worth of vacation banked at work, she had plenty of time to travel. She'd never gone to Mexico to see for herself where Antonio had been, but it had to be now.

If she didn't close this chapter of her life, she could never move on. More than anything, she needed to begin living again.

* * * * *

"Nice digs," Woody commented as they filed into the room Ranger Ops had been given as a sort of home base. It wasn't a Texas Rangers' office, at least,

28

but it was a downgrade even from that. The furnishings were circa 1980s, with chairs sporting metal bases that might have once been modern and now looked like they should be in the dump. Nash's true concern was whether or not the seats would actually collapse beneath all of their weights.

"They're in the process of a remodel," Nash lied through his teeth.

Woody grunted. "The day anything other than the Oval Office gets a remodel is the day I'm sainted."

That had them all chuckling, but not Nash. He waved at the big table for them to be seated. Then he took up his place at the head, bracing his legs wide and folding his arms over his chest as he eyed them all.

"Looks like most of you have healed from any injuries you sustained on that last mission."

The cartel had been little match for a special ops force, especially when Nash had gone berserk with rage after being ambushed by a couple of armed guards. Afterward, he'd heard the voice of Lang in his mind, telling him to get hold of his anger, to stay level-headed.

He had some work to do.

Lennon lifted a hand in a half salute. He'd been the worst of them, splitting his brow open a second time and now sporting stitches. The blackened scab and swelling were gone, at least.

"All right, guys, getting down to business. You know what I saw down in Coahuila. And I have orders for reconnaissance as soon as we can scramble. What is before you is a file with all the information on Antonio Vincent since his disappearance. Study it. Know that shit inside and out, so if something comes up down there, you will make the connections."

The men flipped open their files and began skimming the pages of photos and investigation reports.

"Also, this was just handed to me." Nash lifted a computer tablet. When he swiped the screen, an image came up.

For a heartbeat, he stared at the woman in the photo, a snapshot as she stepped onto a front stoop when she was unawares. Her body was angled, but Nash was able to make out curve after curve. But what really hit him in the solar-plexus was her hair. Thick dark brown that shone red in the sun and waved over one high cheekbone.

His guys were waiting for him to show them the screen, but Nash flicked his gaze over her face a moment before holding it up.

"This woman is Vincent's sister Nevaeh. She's been interrogated at length since his disappearance, as you'll read in the notes. But recently two Texas Rangers visited her and her family, and Miss Vincent recalled another detail." He swiped the screen again, moving to the document of notes that had been scanned into the email. He already knew what was written there, so he passed the tablet to Woody seated on his right.

The man merely glanced at the document before flipping back to the photo of Nevaeh Vincent. He let out a low whistle.

"Damn, she's fucking beautiful. If this is what we get to look at as Ranger Ops, I made the right decision to accept the job."

To Woody's side, Lennon leaned in. "Holy hotness. Are there any more pictures of her? Perhaps in her bra and panties?"

Nash's chest gave a sudden burn of irritation. "Cut it out. Just read your files and what is on that screen while I detail out the plan."

He sank to the chair, and sure enough, the metal legs seemed to dip beneath his weight. He moved gingerly so as not to bend the living fuck out of it and rested his elbows on the table. "With this new bit of information, we believe Vincent might have been involved in some illegal hacking. He was a big techie, a college kid who liked to hike and travel. We confiscated his computer back when he disappeared, but it cannot be found today. It's disappeared as well, maybe discarded as junk. Either way, his hard drive revealed nothing. Of course, if Vincent was skilled, he might have wiped it before he left for Mexico. That in itself raises a lot of questions."

A few of the guys mumbled their agreement as they flipped through the files.

Nash went on. "Recently, I had the authorities searching for the whereabouts of that hard drive, and damn if it wasn't located for me. Jess? This is yours." He held up the small piece of electronics that had been given to him.

"I'll look at it now." Jess had the tablet and was eyeing the photo of the woman. Nash caught a glimpse of her and twisted his gaze away. He had to focus — no time to think of how long it'd been since he'd had a woman in his bed.

A soft, curvaceous woman.

Never one with hair like that, though. Damn, what he wouldn't give to sink his hands into that thick mass while driving into her tight body.

He cleared his throat.

Jess got up and went to the corner where a computer system was set up, as high-tech as they came with all the bells and whistles one would expect from working with the government, even if they didn't give a shit about their office space.

He began to hook up the hard drive and in seconds had something on the screen.

Nash went on, "We're headed to Mexico at O-six-hundred. Destination is a hostel where Vincent was last seen checking in. Lots of kids stay there during spring breaks, and it isn't unheard of for drug deals and the like to go down there. But what we believe we're dealing with isn't a hijacked tourist."

Woody and Cavanagh looked up from their files. "He might have just been buying drugs and got into a bad deal," Cavanagh said.

"Could be. Though Vincent wasn't known to use drugs or alcohol other than an occasional beer. What this new evidence points to — "

Jess broke in, "Is that the bro's got a big fingerprint, and I can follow it."

Nash got up and went to the computer desk. The others followed, all fanning out behind Jess as he brought up a code on the screen. "See this? It's a series of letters and numbers, but it's basically Vincent's signature. Is there anything I haven't read yet in that file about this question of hacking?"

Nash leaned in to examine the codes, which just looked like gibberish to him. "His sister recalled walking in on him while he was online, and there were rows of codes on the screen. When he typed something in, a restricted warning came up, and when he started scrambling, she left in a hurry and didn't see more."

Jess was nodding. "Makes sense. How the hell's this all been missed for what? Ten years?"

"That's right," Nash said.

"Probably were searching in all the wrong places." Woody crowded closer to look at the screen. "They were looking for a kid who went hiking and got lost, maybe slipped into a canyon or was murdered for his possessions and buried in a spot they had no chance of discovering. They weren't thinking he was involved in anything criminal, like hacking into a database that had earned him notice."

"He might have been lured down here," Cavanagh spoke up.

Nash straightened away from the screen. "We've got our work cut out for us. We're not talking about paperwork checks here, guys. We're special forces now, and we have to think like them."

"What's the plan, boss?" Woody already looked ready to roll out.

Nash was too, now that they had more of a handle on what they were looking for, thanks to Jess. "We'll disguise ourselves as tourists and start following any trails we can, talk to people and see if they remember anything or know of any known organizations in the area. People who don't want to be known."

Jess nodded. "That's what I'm seeing here. I need a few hours to really dig, but this kid entered some unknown fucking territory, by the looks of it."

Nash clamped a hand on Jess's shoulder. "Take the time you need."

"Sully?"

He turned at his nickname, modeled off Sullivan.

"Why exactly do we have this?" Linc held up the tablet with the photo of Vincent's sister.

"Because she's said to resemble Vincent in features and coloring. Though the man I saw on the street was wearing a ball cap..." Nash stared at the woman's face. He nodded. "Yeah, that's what he looks like, though obviously she's much more feminine."

Much, much more. But the set of their eyes and the way their lips bowed was undeniably a genetic trait they shared.

"That old photo might not provide the image we need of Antonio. But maybe having this woman's face locked into your brains will help you recognize him once we get down there." He made a fist and bumped it against his lips as he stared at the woman. The Texas Rangers had reported how irritated Vincent's sister had been while speaking to them, and that their mother had gone inside the house in tears.

New determination struck Nash. They were fucking finding this guy and returning him to his life. When Ranger Ops was finished, Antonio Vincent's picture wouldn't be hanging on walls anymore.

Chapter Three

The air was stifling in the bus, and Nevaeh's shirt clung to all the wrong spots. Along the route to Mexico, she'd found a hairband and pulled her hair into a messy topknot, but it did nothing to keep the perspiration from rolling down her neck.

Some of the other passengers had gotten out of their seats to speak to the driver, asking about air conditioning, but he only said it was on. Clearly, it was not. The conditions were miserable, but she was on her way to Mexico and couldn't back out, so she'd just have to deal with her spine sticking to the vinyl bus seat.

Outside the foggy window, the landscape didn't change much between Texas and Mexico — same earth, same types of vegetation that survived with little water during these hot months.

Soon she'd arrive at the same hostel where Antonio had last been seen. She had little idea of what to do once she got there, but she'd figure it out. This was her one chance — her only hope. She didn't put much faith in those Texas Rangers taking renewed interest in the case — after all, she'd been here before. Several times, in fact.

Back at home, she hoped her parents were keeping busy as she'd told them to. Daddy needed to keep working or risk being let go, and it was good for him to get out of the house. Her mother was more difficult.

She'd lost her job after her son's disappearance and had been such a basket-case since that she hadn't been able to hold another position. Nevaeh had suggested her mother work on some of her sewing projects she sometimes took in for people, and her mother had nodded in agreement, but Nevaeh had seen that blank look in her mother's eyes that told her she had shut down again... the sign in the storefront turned to *closed*.

Letting out a sigh, she took a bandanna and wiped at her neck. First thing she'd do when she arrived at the hostel was shower. She needed to feel cool and clean. Then she'd have a look around and formulate a plan.

Across the aisle, a woman had a little girl snuggled on her lap. The child's legs dangled over her thigh, swaying with the movement of the bus. Her thumb was plugged in her mouth and her big brown eyes wide and staring as kids did right before falling asleep.

Nevaeh didn't want to stare, but it was hard not to look at people and see how their lives progressed while she was stuck, in a standstill. After her brother disappeared, she had gone on to graduate from high school, do a stint for business in a community college and land a job at a solid government agency that gave public assistance. But she hadn't truly *lived*.

The woman across from her — she'd found love in the man who sat at her side and they'd shared that bond by creating a child.

Nevaeh had given up dating, and she was well aware of how that wall she'd erected to keep out the pain of her loss had kept out everyone else too. Her ideas of what her adulthood would be like had twisted into a confusing knot that cinched tighter by the year. Lately, she'd begun to wonder if she could ever pick it apart if she had the chance.

The child's eyes dropped shut. After a minute, her mouth went slack and her thumb fell to her lap. The bus went on swaying, the landscape trundling by Nevaeh's window.

Instead of dwelling on the things she couldn't control, she tried to organize her thoughts into things she could. First, she'd have a thorough look around the hostel. Having never been in one before, she wasn't sure what to expect, but stories were that they were places kids went to party on spring break and could sometimes be scary, with seedy people sharing the same bathrooms or rooms being easily broken into and personal belongings stolen.

At least she hadn't brought anything of value with her — a knapsack filled with clothes, her debit card and a very small amount of cash she planned to exchange for some pesos.

She dazed out for a while, her mind wandering over places she'd visit to try to retrace her brother's footsteps that fateful day he'd gone missing. When the bus came to a stop, she jolted into awareness.

Sitting up straight, her back peeled away from the seat, and she stifled a groan. People around her began collecting their items and getting to their feet, and Nevaeh did too.

With her backpack slung over her shoulder, she made her slow way up the aisle to the doors of the bus. The street was busy, milling with tourists and pedestrians. She knotted her bandanna around her throat. Her attire would fit right in with everyone else—loose cotton pants, a tank top and the bandanna. She had comfortable sandals on her feet and nothing about her would stick out, which was what she wanted.

When she reached the steps, she descended and stepped onto concrete. The crowd propelled her on for some time, but soon she got her bearings and took off on foot in the direction of the hostel. She'd studied a map for two straight days so she had enough confidence to make it to her destinations. A lost tourist would be a target, and she didn't want to put herself in a bad situation.

The sights, scents and sounds of the city would be infectious and invite excitement on any other occasion, but Nevaeh's reason for being here was more depressing than these people probably saw in a lifetime. Actually, she hoped that was the case—

nobody should suffer the way she and her parents had this past decade.

Walking the street gave her some new ideas about places to visit and ask about Antonio. A computer shop could perhaps offer some clues, if it had been in business when Antonio had been there, of course.

The hostel she arrived at was painted a bright pink and yellow in keeping with the festive colors of the city. In front was a short block wall painted yellow as well, and a few people sat there talking and laughing.

She approached the door, heart pounding. Is this what Antonio had seen upon coming here? The place looked freshly painted, so she doubted it was this well kept at that time.

Through the front door was an open space that the warm breeze washed through. She welcomed the feel of the breeze on her sweaty body as she stated her name and checked in. She was given a key and the directions to the staircase leading to her room.

The interior was painted a pale blue, and again, she doubted it had been this bright and airy when Antonio visited. At least she'd always imagined someplace seedy, dark and filled with all the wrong sort of people, smoking with needle tracks up their arms.

The thought that she might have been wrong all these years, that her brother hadn't faced dangers she'd imagined, threw her off-balance.

A door in the hallway slammed, and she heard giggles behind it. Locating her own room, she used the key and stepped inside. She'd paid for a private space, but if you had a smaller budget you could share a room with a stranger. That did not appeal — at all — so she'd shelled out a few extra bucks and gladly.

Inside her room, it smelled faintly of grilled corn. She drifted to the window and looked down on a courtyard where some people were grilling. Smoke rose upward, the source of the smell.

Her stomach rumbled. After her shower, she'd find food.

Another glance around the space revealed a simple bed with a white cover. There was no pillow, which she hadn't expected, so she'd need to ask about that. First things first — the shower.

With her knapsack on her shoulder, she went back out into the hallway and found the one bathroom on this floor that many would share. When she entered, a man looked up from the sink where he was brushing his teeth. With the brush sticking out of his mouth, he offered her a smile. She nodded and moved past him toward the showers.

The last thing she wanted was to be raped here, so she had to be watchful. She didn't know these people and would not let down her guard.

Tucking her bag into a corner where she could keep an eye on it from the open shower, she washed quickly and dried off even faster, using a towel she'd brought from home. Then she dressed in a clean pair of jeans and another tank top. This time she tied a bandanna around her hair like a headband but kept the topknot. It was too hot to have all her heavy hair shrouding her shoulders.

Feeling much improved, she went back downstairs and stepped onto the street once more, in search of sustenance. Maybe some grilled corn.

* * * * *

The moment Nash entered the hostel, he sensed a tension hanging in the air. When he and his guys had checked in here earlier, the atmosphere had not been so... what was the word? Guarded.

He gave Woody the side-eye and they peeled off throughout the downstairs common rooms, on high alert. The other guys did the same, fanning themselves in the spaces. To outward appearances, they were just young guys who'd come to Mexico to party. Nash tugged at the collar of his T-shirt, and he couldn't' tell if he was just the heat of the day or the repressed vibe in the place.

He swept his gaze over the room and stopped dead.

His hands fisted at his sides as he spotted that familiar mass of hair bundled into a knot on top of her head. A quick assessment said she was the reason the people were on edge, and as he moved in, he heard why.

The woman was asking questions.

Very pointed questions.

"Have you ever seen this man here or in the city?" She held out a photograph to the young man she was speaking to, and he shook his head. "Have you ever seen people hanging around here that would maybe be of ill repute? Maybe some drug dealers or..."

Jesus Christ. She was going to get herself killed asking shit like that.

Nash swept in and closed his fingers over her upper arm. She looked up sharply, muscles bunching under his hold. He looked into her eyes. Fuck, they were beautiful, like stained glass windows of brown, green and gold.

"There you are. I've been looking for you. C'mon." He pulled her away from the man, and she didn't fight him.

Fuck, she really was vulnerable as hell, and her name would definitely be on the next list of Americans gone missing in Mexico if he didn't get her trusting little ass out of here now.

He stifled a growl that rose into his throat. Towing her several feet away, he threw Woody a look before twitching his head to the door. Woody gave a nod, imperceptible to those not looking for it.

When Nash pulled the woman into the courtyard, he immediately scanned the area for threat. Men on his nine, two young guys shootin' the shit. Not a threat.

The woman in his hold looked up at him with big eyes, and now the stained glass effect shattered as anger filled her stare.

"Who are you? Why did you grab me and drag me out here? I'm not an object to be hauled around where you wish!"

He found himself staring at her mouth. Was it horrible that he wanted to silence her with a kiss? Yes. It was. He wasn't an animal who spotted a pretty girl and thought with his dick.

Pitching his voice low, he said, "I'm doing you a favor, Nevaeh."

She yanked away from him and took two steps before he blocked her path. "Calm down now. I'm here to help you. Protect you. You're looking for your brother, and I am too. But dammit, the questions you're asking are going to get you dragged off in the night and never seen again."

Her eyes flared wide. "How do you know my name? How do you know about Antonio?"

He slanted a look at the guys, who weren't paying attention to them, but Nash wasn't about to risk them catching their conversation. He returned his focus to Nevaeh, and he was stricken anew by her beauty.

No—her goddamn breathtaking appearance. A measure of untouched innocence coupled with a sensuality any man would be hard and aching for if he spent more than five minutes in her presence.

44

Hell, he was counting down the seconds till he popped a boner, and he was a man who was in control.

He had to get her out of here.

"Come with me."

She drew back her shoulders, weighing her options, it seemed.

"Look, I can't tell you more here, but I'm also investigating Antonio's disappearance. Come with me."

She blinked at him. And then she nodded.

Hell, that was just as bad. Because any man could tell a lie and this beautiful, trusting woman would follow him. Nash had to educate her on personal safety while traveling alone in a foreign country, and fast.

He led her back inside. Linc stood off to his right and when he saw who Nash had at his side, his eyes bulged. Nash saw his lips move, and from another room, Lennon entered, summoned through the communication system they all wore.

He realized his wasn't connected and discreetly messed with it until in his own ear, he heard, "Jesus Christ on a kabob. What is she doing here?"

My sentiments exactly.

He didn't speak but led Nevaeh Vincent up the stairs and into the hallway. Which room was hers? How the hell had he missed that she was coming here? Clearly, somebody seated behind a computer on the back end of this mission was not doing their fucking job. She never should have made it out of her hometown let alone across the border. But here she was, standing next to him, more stunning than her photo ever could have revealed.

And playing into a dangerous game.

He tapped once on a door to alert his team he was entering. When he pushed it open, Woody and Jess were hovering over a computer system that stretched across most of one wall of the room. They turned at the same time, eyes bulging.

"I need a minute, guys."

"You can't question her alone. You need another party in the room. Go on, Jess. I'll stay." Woody drifted to a corner and pretended to look out the window while Nash turned to Nevaeh.

She was staring with wide eyes at one of the monitors that revealed surveillance of not only the hostel but every street corner in the city. The differing views flashed on the screen in intervals, all being recorded for closer looks later.

"What is..." Her words trailed off as her stare lit on the computer. Her brother's information was on the screen, a login page with his college grades.

Nevaeh rushed across the room. She touched the screen and then spun on Nash. "What is this doing in your possession? Who the hell are you?"

"It's all right. Calm down. My name is Captain Nash Sullivan. A team of us is trying to track your brother's course he took ten years ago. All this" — he swept his arm over the equipment— "is helping us to do that."

He wasn't saying more, except to impress upon this woman how he was placing her on the next bus back to Texas.

She planted a hand on a very lush hip. "You're here looking for Antonio?"

"That's right. And so are you, but not for long. You're going home, Miss Vincent."

She was shaking her head before the words left his mouth. From the corner, he caught movement, Woody turning with a hand to his mouth as if covering laughter.

Nash took another tack. He waved to the desk chair. "Have a seat, please."

She eyed him warily before sinking to the chair. Nash took a few steps back so as not to tower over her and intimidate. He'd use that to his advantage later if she refused to go again.

"When did you arrive in Coahuila?" he asked.

"This morning."

"You were on a night bus?"

She nodded. That thick knot of hair wobbled on top of her head, and he itched to let down the mass and spread it around her shoulders.

"Why did you come here, Miss Vincent?"

"I'm looking for answers I never had the guts to search for before. Recently some Texas Rangers came—" She cut off, staring at him. "They came to our house asking questions again because of you, didn't they?"

"Because of this mission, yes. Look," he pitched his voice low, "this is sensitive stuff. No one wants to give up information ten years after the fact and finding the people who could tell us anything will take time and skill. You walking into a hostel where your brother checked in a decade ago and questioning the people here will not give you the answers you seek."

She straightened her shoulders, eyeing him. God, she was a strong little thing. Fierce, he'd say, though he hadn't yet seen that put to the test.

Hopefully, he'd have her on a bus before then.

"I advise you to stop asking questions and return home. Let us do our jobs."

She shook her head. Woody's chuckle sounded from the corner, and he sliced a glance his direction. "Miss Vincent, there are people who won't like you asking questions. You have no clue what you'll stumble across here, and you're going to get yourself in deep trouble if you continue."

"I'm prepared for that. I have to find out what happened to Antonio."

"Not to burst your bubble, but do you honestly believe that you can find out what teams of investigators haven't in ten years?"

She narrowed her eyes at him and stood from the chair. He took a step toward her. Compared to him, she was small and delicate. She wouldn't stand a chance against anybody with a mind to hurt her.

Nash couldn't let that happen.

He reached around her to a phone that was unable to be tapped. Bringing it to his ear, he was immediately connected with his guy back in the States who got them what they needed and fast.

"I need the first bus—no, make that a flight—back to San Antonio." She couldn't get off a jet.

"No!" She fisted her hands.

He had a job to do and keeping her safe was his first priority.

"We'll be there. Thanks." He hung up and looked into Nevaeh's eyes. Anger burned there.

I know the feeling, little woman.

"Look, darlin', you don't want to be around here when we actually do find anything out. Go home, go back to your parents and comfort them while you wait for us to give you the final word on what happened to your brother. Okay?"

She dropped her hands and adopted a don't-even-think-about-it stance. "I'm not leaving."

"Yes, you are."

"I'll be fine. I won't get in your way."

"Won't get in our way? Woman, you already have. Those questions you asked have a ripple effect. Pedro will tell Juan who will tell Jose and pretty soon, the whole city knows we are searching for a man who came here ten years ago and never went home again."

She flinched, paling slightly, but did not look away from him.

Yes, fierce.

"You've already thrown up some roadblocks for us to skirt around before we can even begin to do our work. Now, let's go to your room and gather your things. I'm putting you on that flight in an hour."

"I'm not leaving," she stated again.

"You don't know what you're up against."

"Yes, I do. I'll keep out of your way. I'll—"

Grabbing her by the shoulders, he spun her to face one of the screens with a headline and news story of the missing man, who was possibly a lost hiker. Jabbing a finger toward the photo of her brother, he ground out, "That will be you. But you won't be as lucky as your brother."

Under his hand locked on her small shoulder, a tremor ran through her.

"I can help." Christ, her tone didn't sound one bit cowed.

Nash whirled her back to look at him. "He had something to offer somebody. You don't." His words dropped like hard concrete blocks, and he saw a bit of the light go out of her eyes.

Dammit.

But it was for her own good.

His temper was on the rise.

He let her go and looked to Woody. "Look after her. I need a minute."

As Nash strode to the door, Woody intercepted him. "Wait, Sully."

He paused and released a heavy breath through his nostrils. He had to get as far away from that woman as possible. He was reacting to her. Every look, every word she shot his way, felt like a personal attack on his orders. For a minute there, he was actually leaning toward letting her remain here with them.

That was fucking nuts.

Woody leaned in to speak low. "We could use her."

"Fuck, not you too. How? No fucking way. This is our first mission and having a civilian in the way will only fuck it up."

"But we already know Antonio might have been grabbed by someone who is tech savvy. We could use her."

"No," Nash said with force. Damn him for having that quick tactical mind. Nash had thought of it too, but he didn't need anybody trying to talk him into things.

"Let's put her out there on the web and see who she draws in. We'll alter her brother's fingerprint just a touch so the right people will know it's someone who knew him."

"No."

Woody went on, throwing a glance over his shoulder at Nevaeh still staring at the computer screen of her brother's headline. "She can draw someone in."

"If that's your plan, we can do it without her present. Set up the fingerprint but leave her outta this. She's going home."

"Sully. If we set this up, someone is bound to go looking for her. Sending her home will only put her in danger."

Goddammit. Woody was right.

Suppressing a growl of irritation, even he realized this was their best shot at luring in the person they were looking for in the fastest possible way.

Nash walked over to Nevaeh and jerked his head at her. "Let's go."

This time she followed. He led her to a room next to that one, a private room with enough locks to keep her safe. When he closed the door, she wrapped her arms around her middle, drawing his attention to her curves once more.

"You'll be safe here. Where are your belongings? I'll have them brought here."

She stared at the series of deadbolts his team had installed on the door, and then she shifted her gaze to his. The instant he looked into her eyes, a burning took up in his gut.

"I'm not going back."

"You will when we tell you to."

Dammit. He couldn't afford to lose his temper with her. One bellow and she'd crumple. He didn't want that.

"Please. There's nothing at home but dead air and sadness. We're all frozen in time, locked into the moment we first heard Antonio was missing. Every hour since ticks by so slowly." She faltered, glancing down at her feet clad in leather walking shoes. When she met his gaze again, a spear shoved deep into Nash's chest. "I have to try to find him so we can all get our lives back. Even if it's to finally bury his memory."

Any trace of anger fled, and he was left staring at her.

Hell. Now what?

* * * * *

This man—what was his name? She always struggled to remember things when she was upset. She focused on his face, the set of his broad shoulders... and suddenly his name popped into her mind.

Captain Nash Sullivan. The other man in the room had referred to him as Sully.

Nevaeh's mind spun with all the words that had been thrown back and forth in a flurry between she and Sullivan. And yeah, some of it impacted her big time. She hadn't totally considered the sort of trouble she'd be inviting by asking questions. But now she felt stupid for it. She wasn't trained to investigate more than the inside of her closet, her fridge or a shopping mall. What did she think she was doing?

Hanging her head, she debated taking his order to return home. They had a flight ready, and she wouldn't need to spend hours on a dirty bus. She could be home with her parents in hours.

Then again, she had come here seeking closure—one way or another. Even if she agreed to stay out of this Captain Sullivan's way, she would learn the truth quicker by being nearby.

No, she could not go now. Her mind was made up.

Looking at the giant of a man standing before her, she thought she would not be intimidated either. Just because he was big and in charge of somebody—not her—didn't mean she had to listen to him.

He continued to stare at her another long heartbeat, giving her a chance to notice things like a tattoo snaking up his muscle of one arm, mostly covered by his shirt sleeve. And the way his cargo pants hung perfectly low on his hips. Or the little bump on the bridge of his nose that told her it had been broken once.

"Have you eaten?"

His question took her off guard.

"What?"

"Have you eaten recently? I can get you some food."

"I ate lunch."

"That was hours ago." He lifted a hand to his ear and said, "Get us some food here."

She shouldn't be shocked to know he was using some sort of communications device like she'd seen in action movies, yet she was. Somehow, she had landed in something much bigger than she'd ever imagined by coming here. She was facing things she knew nothing about, and frankly, they frightened her a little.

His dark brown eyes were fixed on hers when he said, "Be there in a minute." He reached for the doorknob. "I'll be right back. Lock yourself in and only answer for me. Got it?"

What, now she was a prisoner? Still, what could she do? Either run home or face fears around every corner of the city now that this man had informed her of what could be her fate if she continued snooping on her own.

She nodded.

His brow went up the barest bit, as if he was surprised she'd agreed.

"Lock it behind me," he reiterated before slipping out.

Nevaeh didn't move right away.

"Do it." His harsh voice came through the door, making her jump.

No, this man did not like her very much. The way he spoke to her was enough of a hint to keep her distance from this one. Problem was, the other two men she'd seen in that room weren't much better.

She jumped forward and twisted a deadbolt. When he ground out, "Another," she locked another one.

Listening hard, she tried to hear his footsteps but nothing reached her. She wouldn't put it past a man like that to creep away on silent feet like a mouse, despite his size.

She looked around the room for the first time. This was much like her own, in shades of pastel blue and white. But a dark blind had been pulled over the window, creating all shadows and darkness in the space.

It lent a chill that she hadn't felt in this hostel before, even knowing her brother had been here and never returned. Somehow just knowing he'd passed through those front doors had given her a measure of comfort she rarely felt at home since.

She'd barely gotten her mind to calm down enough to complete a thought when there was a tap on the door. She moved to it, heart thumping. When she listened with her ear to the wood, Captain Sullivan spoke. "It's me. Open the door please."

She did, stepping back as he crowded into the space. But not before she got a breath of his masculine scent.

He swept a look around the room as if expecting to see someone had breached the place since he'd walked out only a few minutes earlier. She moved away from him, needing some distance to think straight. Especially after that scent of musk and pine swirled through her senses.

"Food is on the way."

"Thank you." She pressed her lips together.

"What is it you wish to ask me?" When he looked at her sidelong, it stirred something else inside her, something she didn't want to even think about.

She must be so transparent to a man like him. "I'd like you to explain things better to me."

"What do you want to know?"

"This." She waved at the room. "That." The other room. "Why was my brother's college information on the screen?"

"Because we have his hard drive and are analyzing it."

She blinked. That little box that looked like it was hooked up to life support, with wires and cables projecting from it, had belonged to her brother's computer?

"You told the Texas Rangers who visited you that you'd seen something questionable," he said.

She nodded. "I didn't understand what. I still don't. Have you found something that you believe to be important?"

"I can't share any information with you. All I can say is that we are working on it."

"We."

"My team and I."

"What kind of team? Military?"

"Special ops. We are a division of Homeland Security but while here for another purpose, I spotted something."

"Something." Her heart tripled its beat.

"Someone."

Her jaw dropped, and dizziness swept her. She swayed and clutched onto the nearby chair even as Sullivan reached out for her. His big hand closed around her upper arm, and then he drew her solidly before him, planting his other hand on her shoulder to keep her upright.

"Look, I can't let you hear this on an empty stomach. You're liable to pass out. We'll put this conversation on hold, okay? Here, sit."

He drew her to the chair, which was hard and uncomfy but solid beneath her.

She pressed her fingertips between her eyes, kneading at a headache forming there. "Can I get some water please?"

He nodded and moved to the corner where a mini fridge purred. She hadn't noticed it before, and she was a little disappointed there were drinks right at their fingertips, because she'd hoped for a moment alone.

To think over what he'd just said.

Someone.

Who could that someone be?

Who in the universe could be spotted to tip off a special ops unit to go searching into her brother's disappearance? Only one name came to mind, and it was too much to even hope for, even though her heart was bouncing around in her chest like it was a trampoline.

He handed her a bottle with the cap already twisted off for her. Then a knock sounded on the door, and he moved swiftly to it, hand hovering around his hip, making her wonder what kind of heat he was packing and where he hid such weapons. He was bulked out with muscle, so it wouldn't surprise her if he pulled out a half dozen deadly weapons.

To distract herself, she raised the bottle to her lips and sipped the cool liquid. Sullivan opened the door, spoke quietly to someone and accepted a bag. He twisted no less than three of the deadbolts before turning to Nevaeh.

The scent of fresh tamales reached her, and her mouth watered. Suddenly, she realized just how hungry she was and wet her lips.

Sullivan tracked the action before raising his gaze to hers. "I hope you like tamales. They're fresh."

Her stomach cramped with hunger, and she nodded. "Love them."

A trace of a smile passed over his lips and vanished so quickly she thought she might have imagined it. Then he took the other chair and set the bag on a low table between them. "Help yourself."

She did, reaching for a tamale that was wrapped in paper. When she unrolled it, pure heaven struck her senses, and she moaned. "My grandmother made homemade tamales, and I haven't had one in ages." She quickly peeled back the paper and took a bite. Flavors hit her tongue, so rich that she moaned again.

She took another bite before she realized Sullivan hadn't taken any. "Should I have prayed first or something?"

He chuckled.

The man actually laughed.

She stared at him while he reached into the bag and pulled out a tamale that seemed dwarfed by his sizable hand.

"You can pray if you want. I take it they're good?"

"Mmm-hmm." She took another bite, and he watched her chew as he unwrapped his own. When he bit into it, he gave her a simple nod that didn't tell her what he thought of the flavors of garlic and chiles. They ate in silence a moment. When she'd polished off hers, she reached for another.

"I didn't realize how hungry I was."

"There're plenty."

"What about the other two men?"

He looked at her. "There are six of us, and they can handle themselves. Eat what you want."

"These are almost as good as my grandmother's. She died not knowing what happened to him, you know. I can't let that happen to my parents." Her appetite sank a bit, but she took a bite of the fresh tamale anyway.

"Maybe you can help us."

Nevaeh sat up straighter. "Anything. Just tell me what and I'll do it."

His stare was heavy. "Be careful what you agree to, Miss Vincent. You have no idea what we're asking."

Chapter Four

Nevaeh stared at the paper that was as blank as her mind. Captain Sullivan had told her they were trying to figure out a certain coded password string to get into one section of a program on Antonio's hard drive. The captain had left her with a pen and paper and the instructions to write down all she could think of, important or not.

What to write?

She pressed the point of the pen into the sheet but couldn't come up with a single word. She gave up and went to the window. Lifting the dark blind, she peered out at the city. People milled everywhere, and laughter reached her, a faint sound carried on the breeze.

Being here was like a dream, but not of the good variety. Visiting as a tourist, she could only imagine how excited her brother had been.

A knock on the door had her crossing the room.

"It's me. Open up."

She did, standing back farther this time, giving the big captain all the room he needed. He crowded in with her backpack and set it down.

"You'll be staying here from now on, so we can keep you protected." He glanced at the abandoned paper and pen, and his brows crinkled when he saw it was blank.

"I don't know what to write down," she said, biting her lip.

His dark eyes followed the movement, latching onto her lip for a split second before darting back up to her eyes. "Anything you can think of about his life. Hiking, friends' names, college hangouts, the birthday of a girlfriend."

She stared at him, still blank.

"Anything might help us, Nevaeh. I mean, Miss Vincent."

"You can call me by my name."

He nodded but did not offer for her to address him by his. Nash. When she looked at him, the name fit him like a pair of worn leather boots. A little bit country, a lot manly. She wondered how he'd gotten into this position. But another question pushed at the forefront of her brain.

"Can I ask you something?"

"Depends." His voice was no-nonsense. Yeah, he definitely didn't like her much.

"You said you saw someone." She bit her lip again. "My brother?"

"The resemblance was there, yes. But it's been ten years since that photo was taken."

"But you were certain enough to call a team together to investigate it."

He paused a heartbeat before nodding.

Nevaeh's knees weakened, and she moved to sit down. When she leaned forward with her head in her hands, Nash came over too.

Then something happened that hadn't in years— her tears were right there, at the rims of her eyes.

Without lifting her head, she asked, "Can you describe him to me?"

He didn't move, just stood there and didn't speak either.

She looked up.

The man pressed his lips into a hard line before sitting. "Same build. Maybe a bit slumped now. Wearing cargo pants and a black ball cap."

"You didn't see his hair?"

"No."

"Antonio was known for his curly hair. Girls loved to run their fingers through it, and my father would always make fun of him for it."

Nash watched her but didn't say a word.

She made a sound in her throat. "And his face?"

"I saw him full on. He was about to step off a curb and was looking my direction for traffic."

She blinked rapidly, finding her eyes wet. There was no stopping the tears now. They began to flow down her cheeks.

"Look, I don't want to get your hopes up. It could still be a mistaken identity. That's what we're here to find out."

"But you have enough evidence to warrant being here," she pressed.

His stare was a heavy weight on hers. "We do."

"Then I'd better do my part, as I said I would." She picked up the pen but had to dash her tears away with her fingertips in order to see the paper clearly. Leaning forward on the chair, she began to form words. Simple things, starting with Antonio's nickname on the baseball team, his favorite teddy bear's name and so on. When she looked up at Nash, she'd filled half a sheet in a long column of writing.

"Keep going," he said, standing. His big body unfolded with so much grace for his size. "I'll be back to check on you."

"Wait."

He paused, nearly to the door after only two strides.

"Can I open the blind please? It feels so closed off in here."

His gaze flashed to the window and then back to her. It traveled down over her body and slowly back up, leaving her with a tingling awareness.

Men looked at her often, but she ignored them all, having little place in her life for dating or even flirting. But of course Nash wasn't looking at her body that way—he was probably assessing her likelihood of escaping through the window or some similar tactical maneuver.

She waited.

His gaze slid to the bed and then back to her. A warmth crawled over her skin, spreading over her breasts and puckering her nipples from a mere look. She crossed her arms over her chest to keep him from seeing her reaction, and his eyes hardened again.

Finally, he gave a nod. "Just make sure the blind's closed if you undress."

Her eyes widened, but he was already turning for the door. He disappeared and closed it behind himself. It took her a stunned moment to move forward and twist the locks into place again. She didn't hear him move away from the door this time either.

What the...? Why in the world would he care if she undressed with the blinds cracked? As if anybody could even see through the thin slats when she was on the second story. Besides, on the street were plenty of beautiful women, half-dressed in the tropical climate in shorts and crop tops or short barely-there slip dresses.

Nobody would be looking at her. And why would Nash care in the first place?

The mystery was about as unsolvable as her brother's had been for the past decade. Nevaeh sat again and began writing down everything that popped into her head.

It wasn't until the room grew dark with evening light that she realized she'd forgotten to crack the blind at all. Feeling too worn out and stressed to care at this point, she lay curled on her side on the bed.

Her mind formulated the image Nash had relayed to her. Her brother with slightly slumped shoulders, from the wear and tear of his life, in cargo pants and a black ball cap, all that beautiful curly hair hidden away from anybody who might recognize it.

But that hadn't stopped Nash. The man had still put two and two together, and now here they were, searching for Antonio.

Her hopes had never been high, even in the first few hours after they'd learned her brother had gone missing. Something told her that they'd never find him. And now... she was actually feeling the first stirrings of what could only be called hope.

Looking at the computer setup in the other room, at the two men she'd seen who made up the special ops unit and Nash himself... Well, she was as close to hope as she could be.

If anyone could find Antonio, it was them. Hopefully, something she'd written down would aid their efforts and she would finally feel less helpless. After so many years, she hardly remembered anything else.

* * * * *

67

Nash looked around at the busy streets of Coahuila. He'd never been much for traveling or crowds. Born and raised a Texas boy, having grown up between his granddad's ranch and his uncle's, he was more at peace with cattle than anything else. But in law enforcement, he worked with the public on a daily basis.

He'd also spent a long time working on his temper. Early on in his career, he'd had some run-ins with various criminals that had gotten him reprimands on toning it down. But he couldn't help it—he'd been raised in black and white. To him, there weren't shades of gray. You were either on the right side of the law or wrong. Go far enough onto the wrong side, and he was gonna let you know.

Patience, Lang preached into his mind. His buddy had done more for helping him find that grip on control than even his own momma had. The way Lang put it, it had taken Nash years to become a Texas Ranger in the first place, and that meant he *had* the patience it took—he just had to tap into it.

It was true, he'd spent years qualifying for and working as a Texas State Trooper as the first requirement, as well as many physical and mental examinations. He'd gone through countless yearly trainings with specialists and even Army Rangers.

He was fit to subdue this crowd of tourists all milling around in the town's square, but damn if he wasn't itching to get out of the throng.

Dressed in cargo pants and a shirt with palm trees on it, he fit right in. Except he was rigged with his comms unit, had his weapon tucked against his spine and a lethal knife in his hiking boot.

"You should open some of those shirt buttons, Nash. Some pretty girls are eyein' you." Woody's voice filled his ear.

Nash grunted, not bothering to look around at any pretty girls. He could argue that he was on the job and not here for pussy, but fact was, he couldn't imagine a single one of them was more beautiful than the woman who was being guarded back in the hostel.

"Keep an eye out for any drug deals, guys who might be cartel or mafia."

"I know," he ground out at Woody's words.

"All right, all right. Just sayin'. Don't get your thong in a twist."

"You're an asshole. Shut up for a while, will ya?" Nash bit back a smile as he scanned the crowded street.

"I'm no more of an asshole than you are, Sully. Wait. You're coming up on a person of interest." Woody had positioned himself in a high building and had eyes on everything, with the help of binoculars.

Nash felt a muscle tense all the way down his spine. He fixed his gaze on a man ahead of him.

"The navy shirt?"

"That's the one."

"Moving closer." Casually, he wandered around a group of people to draw up behind the man. Right off, Nash saw he was packing. The way he moved as if the weapon was digging into his hip was obvious. But carrying a concealed weapon wasn't a crime in itself, no matter the laws down here. It didn't necessarily make the man a threat—just cautious.

Still, something about him had stuck out to Woody, and Nash had to investigate.

The man veered off across the street, and Nash hung back a bit to survey him. As he reached a group of rough men, the guy held out a hand to clasp one of the other's in greeting. They spoke in rapid-fire Spanish.

"Hope you're as fluent as I've heard you are," Woody said.

"I am," he responded, listening closely to their talk.

To keep from being noticed, Nash slowed his pace, letting people bump into him from all sides as he held up the flow of traffic. The air was rich with food from vendors, and live music played down the street.

Suddenly, a man stepped up beside Nash and didn't move.

Instantly on guard, he threw a glance sideways.

"Jesus Christ," he said under his breath. If anybody could fly under his radar, it was this man. "What the fuck're you doin' here?"

His brother Penn.

Kicked out of the Rangers for a misstep and now out for hire, doing his own vigilante crime fighting.

Penn shot him a cocky grin and then tipped his jaw toward the men Nash was monitoring. "Sure you know what you're doing, bro?"

Only separated by a year in age, they were always rivals.

Without moving his stare off the men, and with his ear still cocked their way to drink in every word they exchanged, he drawled out, "Maybe not. Maybe I should have followed in your footsteps, went beyond protocol to get information to put a case to bed and ended up tossed out for it."

Penn only grinned. Fucker.

An odd affection rose up in Nash, mingled with a healthy amount of irritation. "Stop with your shit and go away or help."

"I'll help."

"Good. Dickhead."

Penn reached out and they bro-hugged. In Nash's ear, Woody chuckled. "Tell him to come up to the room for some margaritas later."

Nash didn't respond to that, because the suspects were on the move. He took off at a slow pace, meandering behind and hiding himself in the crowd so he wasn't obvious.

The guys walked several blocks and entered a building. Nash took note of the address and

71

surroundings. It wasn't residential or office space, and with no puca-shell necklaces, colorful hats or flip-flops, nothing about the front of the place invited tourists.

"Boarded up windows seems like a red flag to me," Penn muttered.

"Thinking the same."

"You gonna follow them in?"

"Get off my dick, would ya? No, I'm not. Woody, you got eyes on this?"

"Not eyes, but I know your coordinates, Sully. Jess is doing a workup now in the system."

Nash and Penn moved down the street a bit, and Nash pretended to look at his phone while Penn took out a cigarette that he didn't light.

"Building is owned by a Sofia Aricelli. Used to serve as a general store back in the eighties. Now it stands empty." Woody grunted in Nash's ear. "Maybe those guys are starting a business again."

Nash drifted back toward the building, trying to see through a crack where the boards didn't quite cover the entire window. "Bullshit. Get Jess on this. Any police reports in the area, relatives of the owner."

"Already on it. Might as well head back to the party, Sully. Lots happening in the square now. There's a fight breaking out."

"Not yet." Nash stepped up to the door and knocked on it.

Penn let out a laugh and pocketed the unlit cigarette. "Didn't know you had it in ya, brother."

"I got a feeling about this place. Keep your mouth shut and let me do the talking."

He knocked again, and this time one of the men came to the door. His dark eyes slid from Nash to his brother and back to Nash. "No tourists," he said in stilted English.

In Spanish, Nash said, "I'm looking for someone who knows about computers."

"No computers. Go away."

"A friend of mine told me you have ways of fixing computers here that others do not," Nash pressed on in fluent Spanish.

The man shook his head. "I don't know what you're speaking of. Now go."

Nash turned to Penn. Still speaking the native tongue so the man at the door understood, he said, "Didn't Dom say this is the place we should go?"

"Si."

"If he's sending us on a dead errand, I'm going to put his balls in a meat grinder."

Not being as quick with Spanish, Penn didn't follow but just nodded enthusiastically. Nash pretended to get worked up, cussing and looking around the street, spewing things about getting information out of a computer that nobody else had been able to.

The man at the door watched him closely. Nash swore something slithered behind his eyes, but he wasn't biting—he shook his head and slammed the door in their faces.

Nash cursed loudly in Spanish and then walked away with Penn at his side.

"Nice job. You got him interested," his brother said.

"Thanks. How the fuck are you operating here in Mexico with your Spanish being so bad?"

"I got other ways of talkin'." He touched his side where his weapon was concealed. "That guy knew what you were looking for."

"I know." Nash rounded the corner and spotted Cavanagh.

"What's that mangy dog doin' here?" Penn said.

Nash tossed him a look. "For a PI you don't know fucking much, do you? We're working together. Split off from me and circle the block. Meet up here." He handed Penn a matchbook with the logo of a bar next to the hostel on it.

"Thanks for the light," Penn called to Nash's retreating back.

Amusement struck Nash, along with that familial warmth of seeing his kid brother again. He shook his head, but his smile didn't fade. "Asshole," he muttered.

Woody snorted in his ear. "Brotherly love."

* * * * *

Nevaeh had chewed off all her fingernails. She'd chewed bite marks into the end of the pen. And she'd eaten far too many leftover tamales.

She seriously needed to get a grip on needing to put things in her mouth when she was anxious. At least there wasn't a stash of her favorite dark chocolate sitting around the room, because she'd gain ten pounds by the time she made it home.

Home. What were her parents doing? Was she going to give them the news they needed to move on with their lives? All she wanted was for them to begin living, to see some smiles on their faces more often.

She opened the door of the mini fridge, but the tamales were gone and only bottled waters remained. She grabbed one and kicked the door shut.

This room was becoming claustrophobic. First thing this morning, Nash had come in, gotten the paper she'd scribbled on half the night and then moved back to the door in that predatory rolling walk of his. Right before leaving, he'd cast her a hard look over his shoulder. "Stay put. We're keeping an eye on you."

She couldn't quite figure that out either—was she being held prisoner? Nobody had come in to explain it to her, and the one time she'd cracked the door hoping to go out, she was met with the back of a huge man, almost as tall and muscled as Nash.

Nash—when had she begun thinking of him by his given name and not a captain or Sullivan? She was really starting to lose her mind in here.

Another thing that had been eating at her were the words she'd written down… and one she hadn't.

A nickname her brother had used for her since the day she was born. Baby deer. Or baby dear. The terms were interchangeable. As a child, he'd probably meant it as a sweet term, but as he'd grown and developed a sense of humor, he'd drawn pictures of her as an actual fawn and his first gift to her purchased with his own money had been a stuffed deer.

She'd loved that deer to death, dragging it around by one leg until it hung by threads and her mother had to sew it. The stuffed toy had earned a special place on her bed, and every time she looked at it, she thought of Antonio.

For an hour she'd been battling with a plan that had formulated in her mind. It was a bad idea, right? Yet she couldn't shake it. Finally, she walked to the door and opened it.

The man was still standing there, broad back to her, arms folded over his chest. When he half-turned to look at her, she followed the bulge of his biceps to his forearms snaked with cords of sinew and veins.

She looked up at him. Man, he was tall. Was Nash really this large?

Larger, her brain reminded her.

"Um, would you like some water?" She offered him the unopened bottle.

"No thanks."

"Uh… I'm hungry. Would you be able to grab me something to eat?" She wasn't really, still stuffed with tamales. But she hoped her plan to lure him from her doorway worked and she could sneak out.

"Sure. Do you have any preferences?"

She shook her head, hiding the leaping of her heart. It was working.

"No, I'm not picky. Anything will do. Thank you."

"Sure thing." He moved away from her door and went to the other.

Crap, it wasn't going to work. He wouldn't just leave her unguarded, not if he had orders, and she knew he must.

Just before he reached for the door, he turned his head and stopped. It took her a moment before realizing someone had spoken to him through his communication device.

He opened the other door and poked his head in to say something.

Nevaeh took her chance and slinked out of the room, hurrying around the corner where the stairs were and praying she wasn't seen by one of the special ops unit Nash captained. She didn't want to know what the man would have to say about her hiding from those meant to protect her.

Listening hard over the pounding of her own heart, she heard heavy footsteps. For a moment, she had a jolt of fear that the men were headed her way. But they were moving the opposite.

They walked to the end and Nevaeh rushed to the door of the room with the computer setup.

Briefly listening for voices, she kept a watch on the hallway. A young girl exited a room with a giggle, and Nevaeh was shocked by the sound. What a different world that young woman was living in while she was deeply involved in this darker, scarier one.

Well, she either opened the door or didn't. If she didn't hurry, she'd be caught—those men were standing with their backs to her but could turn at any second.

She needed that laptop and standing here wasn't going to make it magically appear in her hands.

She twisted the handle. Part of her expected to find the door locked, but it wasn't. Heart pounding wildly, she peeked her head inside. Nobody was in sight, but she knew that space wasn't unpatrolled and open. Someone was in there, but she needed to slip past him.

She darted in, eyes on the prize. A laptop was still hooked up to her brother's hard drive. She quickly unplugged the power cord and ran for the door.

When she slipped back into the space she'd been ordered to stay hidden in, she leaned on it, breathing heavily as if she'd run a marathon when it had been no more than a few steps.

Dumb luck had been on her side, and she hadn't been caught.

Yet.

She gripped the laptop to her chest and reached behind herself to twist two deadbolts. It was only a matter of time before one of the guys realized what was missing from their computer setup and come looking for her. Until then...

Rushing to the bed, she opened the laptop. It took a second for the screen to pop up, but there it was — all the words she'd written had been punched in rows and were even now processing, blinking on the screen as each was tried against the hard drive.

With no clue what she was doing or even looking for, she added another to that list.

Cría de ciervo.

Baby deer.

Suddenly, the laptop began beeping. Windows opened. Nevaeh's jaw dropped as she stared. Then a loud buzzing tone filled the room.

Loud thumping at her door raised a half-scream from her, and she launched off the bed, staring at the laptop as if it was about to explode.

"Nevaeh! Let me in!"

That deep voice made her heart slam harder. The laptop continued to buzz in that alarming way.

She launched off the bed and ran to unlock the door. Nash and another guy burst in. His gaze landed on the laptop, and he stormed to it, muscles throwing off vibes of his power.

He spun to glare at her. "You stole this from the other room."

"I—"

"Damn, she's a beauty," the other guy remarked.

Nash growled and stalked over to Nevaeh. He grabbed her by the upper arms and hauled her onto tiptoe. "You stole that and brought it in here. What did you enter into it to make it start up those programs?"

Suddenly, two other men appeared in the doorway. One rushed to the laptop, scooped it onto his thighs and began typing madly. The alarm silenced in seconds, leaving her ears ringing and allowing her to hear just how erratically her heart tripped.

"Of course she's got eyes only for Nash," the guy she'd never seen before commented in an amused way.

"Shut the fuck up, Penn. Get out."

The man only laughed.

As tough as she wanted to be, she dropped her gaze from Nash's direct one.

"What did you do? Tell us now."

"I... I entered another word into the passcode list."

"Jesus. She tapped it. She fucking did it." The man looked over the laptop at them.

Nash spun her to the bed, holding her there. "Point to the word."

It wasn't the last word, but one she'd entered into the middle of a column. With a shaking finger, she pointed to it.

"My Spanish is good, but that is the oddest password I've ever seen." The man shook his head as if in awe.

Nash read it and yanked her around to face him. "Fix it, Jess. I need to talk to Miss Vincent alone."

She found herself hauled into yet another room, this one with what appeared to be bulky bags holding what she could only think must be weapons. Nash closed the door and locked it.

She was officially trapped with this very big, very angry special ops unit captain. He was supposed to be finding her brother, and what she'd done could have forever put a halt to that.

His eyes drilled into her. "What is baby deer?"

"I… It's me. My brother used to call me that. It was a joke between us."

His jaw worked as if he was grinding his teeth. "You should have written it down on the sheet. My men are more experienced to handle what just happened."

"What did just happen?" She angled her head to look up at him, though she could barely meet that

81

heated stare. Funny things were happening to her body again—that warmth was back.

"You breached another system, and they know it. They're tracking us right now."

"Oh no." She felt faint.

"I could have you thrown in jail for interfering in this case."

"I-I didn't mean to cause trouble. It was just something that popped into my head, and I wanted to try the word."

"Then you should have told one of the team to enter it. Jesus, do you have any fucking clue what you're facing here? Somebody snatched your brother because of this. For all we know, they've forced him into slavery for the past decade and have him hacking systems all over the fucking world for God knows what ends."

Her head swirled. Finally hearing what this team suspected had happened to her brother made her stomach sink.

"What about your parents?" Nash barked out. "Do you think losing you to this crusade of finding their son will make life any better for them? Jesus." He grabbed her by the arms, lifted her against him and kissed her.

Slamming his mouth hard over hers, leaving her gasping.

Her body lit in a blaze of want at his mere taste, and she responded by parting her lips.

He washed his tongue through her mouth, seeking, demanding. Her knees weakened, but it didn't matter because he held her fast to his big, steely chest. Her fingers twisted in his shirt but brushed over coarse, springy hair sticking from the opening at the neck.

Nash angled his head and drank from her for long, dizzying seconds before letting her go. She landed back on the heels of her shoes, swaying.

He stared at her, chest heaving. Then he picked her up and spun for the bed. Her body, already ignited, burned hotter as scorching lava slid through her lower belly and down between her thighs. He pressed her back, fitting his hips between her legs, the bulge in his pants nudging hard at her neediest spot.

She cried out, and he caught her hand, pressing it up and over her head to the bed. His eyes darkened even more as he gazed down at her. When he trailed a fingertip from the corner of her mouth, branding her with the rough, callused pad, down her throat and to the crest of her breast, she shivered uncontrollably.

All of a sudden, he pushed away, leaving her alone on the bed while he towered over her. He mashed his fingers through his dark hair. "Fuck, I can't."

She dragged herself to her feet to face him, shuddering as desire pulsed through her system. His deep chocolate eyes only heightened her need as he stared at her with unadulterated lust.

Without a word, Nash pivoted and strode out, leaving her clinging to the reality of what had nearly happened just now.

What she wanted to happen with everything in her being.

* * * * *

Dammit to hell, Nash didn't even have time to hide his boner after that encounter, because the instant he stepped foot out of the room, Cavanagh and Penn were in his face.

He took one look at his brother and his scowl deepened. "Why are you still here?"

"Brotherly love," Penn jibed to Cavanagh.

"We need to discuss some things." Cavanagh rubber-necked as a pretty coed walked down the hall to her room. She glanced back over her shoulder at him, a smile on her face.

Nash shoved a finger into Cavanagh's chest. "No fucking around on missions. Got it?"

Fuck, what a hypocrite he was.

He pushed past the guys and into the room that was serving as their central base. The rest of the team was gathered around the computer station with Jess at the helm.

"She got it. She actually fucking cracked this code, and we're in." Linc turned to look at Nash as he entered. "It wasn't in the plan, but your little Miss

Vincent helped us slide right into the database we needed."

Nash bristled. "She's not *my* little Miss Vincent. What have we got?" He stared at the screen Jess was pointing at. After a second of ingesting the info, he pushed out a breath of surprise. "It fucking *was* those guys in that building we visited today." He turned to Woody.

Shaw Woodward looked like a bodybuilder who'd accidentally put on the wrong set of clothes in the locker room—the polo shirt with big splotchy flowers on it stretched tight over his chest and biceps. And his shorts were... well, stupidly short. Nash would laugh at him if he wasn't so damn distracted by not only what was up on the screen and everything it could mean to locating Antonio and closing this mission fast, but from the one and only little Miss Vincent.

Damn her, why did she have to be so alluring, sexy, stunning *and* taste like pure fucking sin all in one? To a man like Nash, she was goddamn perfect.

And he'd damn near stripped her down right then and there and tasted every delicious inch of her body. The way she'd kissed him back, as if she'd been holding back for days too, still had him sporting wood.

Focus. He had to focus.

"Tonight we're going back there. Get eyes on that building, Jess, and I want every single name and background of every person who goes in and out of it." Nash looked around and settled his gaze on Penn.

"I'm at your service, brother," Penn said.

Nash's first instinct was to send him away, back to whatever hole in the ground he'd come from and let them do their jobs. But fact was, Penn was damn good at what he did, rooting some of the most notorious criminals out of their hiding spots, that they could use him to their advantage.

"Cav, fill in Penn on all that's been happening."

"Gotcha, boss."

While Cavanagh and Penn moved to the table where several pizza boxes sat, Nash gestured to Linc and Woody to come closer. "I'm guessing the database we breached is what? Credit card numbers? Bank accounts?"

"Some yeah," Linc told him, rubbing at the scar above his eye. "Some's a little more worrisome, according to Jess."

Nash didn't want to interrupt their tech guru as he was deep in thought, brows pinched while he typed with manic speed, but he needed to know everything.

"What are we looking at, Jess?" he asked.

"Uh..." He finished typing a series of numbers and then half-turned in his chair to fix his gaze on Nash. "This is a broad scope of data theft, but it extends to government."

"Which government? Mexican?"

He nodded. "That and more. Some Argentinian, Brazilian."

"Show me."

Nash spent the next half hour poring over the information Jess shared with him. When he gathered the guys together, he said, "We've gotta formulate a plan of action."

"I say we storm that building and scope it out to find Vincent. Take all the tech we see and confiscate it. Anyone who tries to stop us, we subdue," Penn drawled, arms folded casually across his chest.

"Like we haven't already considered that, Penn. Besides, you're not part of this team, so you don't get a say."

Penn flipped him off, and everyone laughed, even Nash.

Things were coming to a head faster than he'd expected, thanks to Nevaeh's interference. His mind began to wander over to the woman that Lennon was guarding.

Nash continued, "These guys aren't going to just let us walk in and tear down their entire empire. Besides, it isn't only operated out of that building. Setups like this are much broader. Here's what I'm thinking..."

As he spoke, he made sure the guys were listening. They added ideas, and Nash weighed the options. In the end, the fact was, Nevaeh was still a key player in this dangerous game. And that meant they needed to up the security surrounding her.

"I'm going to steal that fingerprint Nevaeh left behind when she hacked their system. Then I'm going to taunt these assholes." Jess's face lit up at the idea.

"Yeah, do that. Cav, get Lennon and fill him in."

Cavanagh, arms crossed and legs in a wide stance, cleared his throat. "I couldn't help but notice the floor of this hostel has cleared out. You have anything to do with that, Sully?"

He eyed Cavanagh. "What do you think?" He couldn't risk anybody seeing more than what they should and ordered the rooms emptied at once.

He grinned. "You work behind the scenes, but I see you, man." He did a finger wave and walked out.

Nash turned to the rest of the group. "Woody, you're headed downtown to keep an eye on that building. We need more than cameras on it. Linc, you and Penn get to act like a couple of drunk guys talking about your bitcoin wealth and where to spend it or how to invest."

Linc gave a crooked grin. He looked to Penn. "Know anything about bitcoin?"

"No, but I put away a gun runner who was pretty deep in it."

Nash stared at his brother a moment. He might not go about things in an official manner, but he got assholes off the streets, and that was worth something in this world. He squeezed Penn's shoulder and bumped fists with Linc. "Watch each other's six."

"You know it," Linc responded.

Nash moved to the door too.

"I suppose he gets to protect the pretty girl," Penn remarked to Linc.

"Hardest job there is. Holding back from touching all that hair? Hell, I'd rather walk into that building unarmed." Linc cocked a grin.

Nash paused. "Actually, I'm going to move her."

Linc's brows rose. "We look like tourists to anyone on the outside, man."

"I'm still moving her. She isn't safe here, and we need to stay ten steps ahead of anybody who'd come looking. I'll be in touch."

Also, best to ignore the comments about how beautiful she was. His body was already reminding him.

Hell.

He went into the empty hallway and nodded to Cavanagh and Lennon standing outside Nevaeh's door, heads bent together. Despite the hostel being emptied of its guests, the guys weren't speaking aloud. Cavanagh was using a series of hand gestures to get across most of the information to Lennon.

"I'll take over guard duty from here," he said to them.

They gave dual nods of agreement and moved back to the room with the others.

This time Nash didn't knock to get Nevaeh to open the door. Instead, he used several keys on the various deadbolts his men had installed. When he quietly pushed open the door, his gaze fell over Nevaeh lying on the bed, facing away from him. Tenderness shouldn't hit him like a damn tidal wave, but it fucking did.

He also felt her nearness like a kick to the gut.

He closed the door and twisted the locks—all of them.

Fuck, this couldn't be good, but he was drawn to her like nothing else in this world.

He was here to move her, nothing else, and he'd do well to remember that.

He opened his mouth to wake her and ask her to gather her belongings for the trip, when her voice reached him, a warm, soft stroke to his senses.

"I don't want to see you, Captain Sullivan." She didn't look around at him.

"How'd you know it's me?" He walked toward the bed.

"The sound of your footsteps. I really don't want to see you."

He looked down at her. "Too bad." Unable to help himself, he dragged her up off the bed and sat on the edge of the mattress, pulling her onto his lap.

She was stiff in his arms, and no wonder. He'd kissed her, got her to a state of burning and then left her quivering and wanting. He was still aching after the encounter, and she must be too.

"Nevaeh, look at me."

She wouldn't, so he pinched the point of her chin lightly and drew her face up to meet his gaze. "This is a precarious situation we are in," he began.

She nodded. "I shouldn't have stolen that laptop and entered that code."

"It's not that, though you should have told one of us what you were thinking first. That database you breached... those men know what happened."

When she sank her teeth into her lower lip, his cock surged against his fly. "Can they track the location? I know computers can be tracked by their IP addresses..."

"No," he said at once. "Jess disabled all that. But you've left a pathway for them to follow, and we're going to guard you closer from now on. We're going to move you — probably even a few times to ensure you're safe."

"I see."

"This is no picnic for you, darlin'." He couldn't send her back home now, though. Not with the hounds of hell broken loose. She was safer here with him.

Dammit, she was warm and soft in his arms.

The sweet, delicate woman straightened her shoulders with all the determination of a battle-worn soldier. "I can handle it. I just want to find my brother."

His gaze drifted over her beautiful features. "And we're closer than ever now, thanks to you. We will find him, alive or dead." Too late he realized how his words affected her. While she didn't shed a tear, her eyes widened, giving off the stained glass effect again.

Fuck, they were tied together by some invisible rope that could not be cut.

She was staring at his mouth, long lashes dipping to cloak her eyes from him. "Nash. Why did you kiss me?"

A rumble vibrated his chest. "Because I was weak," he grated out.

Her eyes flashed up at him. "Then you wanted to kiss me?"

"Darlin', no one makes me do anything I don't want to. Yes, dammit, I wanted to kiss you, touch you, feel you clench around me—" He broke off, aware of his arousal poking into her round little ass in his lap. What had possessed him to hold her like this? The minute he'd touched her, that steely outer layer she kept locked around herself seemed to have fallen away. Like this, with her cuddled close, she seemed so vulnerable, and he needed to offer comfort, to protect and soothe.

Another fucking misstep, and he couldn't make more mistakes.

But the way she was looking at him, as if she wanted him to kiss her again, had him tilting her face up to his.

"Nevaeh, you fuck with my control."

"I'm sorry." She didn't sound a bit sorry, which would have made him smile if he wasn't in total pain, holding himself back this way.

"Nash."

"Yes?"

"You fuck with my control too." She leaned forward, shocking him by brushing her lips across his. The scantest of touches that ripped apart his world. A fucking grenade would have the same effect on his person.

He grabbed her, latching a hand on her ass and yanking her against his erection even as he cupped her nape and dragged her down to plunder her mouth.

The kiss had no warmup time at all—going from zero to a million degrees of hotness in a blink. She moaned against his lips, and he tugged her closer, deepening the kiss by sinking his tongue deep in her mouth. When she touched the tip of hers to his own, he let out a barely harnessed groan.

Pleasure tore through him, and before he knew it, he was angling her down to the mattress and her breast was in his palm. She arched upward to meet his touch, and he felt her nipple pucker under his hand.

Christ, she was so open to him. Why? What was it about them being alone together that brought this out in both of them? He couldn't imagine Nevaeh was a woman who gave herself to men easily. Hell, her file had reported her as single most of her life.

He ran his hand over her breast again, and she laced his fingers with hers, holding him there. "Touch me, Nash. I've never needed touched so bad."

"Fuck, darlin'. Why me?"

"Because you're the only man who's ever..." she searched for words, "unlocked me." With her fingers still threaded through his, she guided his hand down her torso, letting him explore the dip of her waist before she led him straight to her pussy.

Through her thin leggings, he felt her scorching heat, and his cock pressed up out of the elastic of his boxer briefs. Fuck, he was going to strangle his cock if he didn't get it out soon. But the minute he did, it would be all over—he'd claim her in every goddamn way a man could, and that was much scarier than facing a firing squad for his actions.

Because he couldn't have her. Couldn't keep her. He was crossing so many lines, it was a sure court martial for his behavior. His actions would be construed as taking advantage of a vulnerable relative to the man they searched for.

Yet, he couldn't quit touching her.

He skimmed his hand over her pussy, learning the swollen feel of her outer lips through her clothing, which was quickly growing damper. She moaned into his mouth, and he gave up to it.

"Touch me, Nash. Please." Her words sank into his brain, and he was helpless against her plea. He yanked back to look into her eyes. "Fuck, I can't stop it. I have to have you."

* * * * *

Nevaeh had never touched muscles like Nash's. Spanning her hands over his shoulders was enough to fuel her fantasies for years, so when she pulled off his shirt and laid eyes on the rest of that chiseled torso... She ran her tongue over her lower lips, and he let out an answering rumble in his chest.

"I like how you look." Her voice sounded breathless, but no wonder with those pecs looming in front of her vision.

The corner of his mouth tipped upward, but the gesture was gone as soon as it came, a fleeting moment of the true man beneath all this rugged exterior. He was a fighter, a protector. She wanted to know more about him, but she knew her body connected with his on a primal, instinctive plane.

Resting her fingers on his chest, she began to explore as he kissed her senseless. Each dip of his tongue into her mouth sent her up another dizzying

95

notch, and the muscled steel beneath her fingertips edged her toward a frenzy.

He skimmed his hands over her waist, latching onto her hips briefly and bringing them up against his in the slightest of bumps that ignited. This man knew how to tease and unravel her.

Passion spread, and she hitched her thigh around his hip, grinding lightly.

"Easy, darlin'," he drawled out in that Texas boy way. "Take it slow."

"Nash," she arched as his lips skated into her cleavage. He yanked her top down to expose the swells of her breasts to his scorching hot tongue. Each lick and swirl had her gripping at him and rocking upward. Hooking a finger into her bra cup, he tugged aside the cloth and swiped his tongue over her nipple.

"Oh gawwwwd." She shuddered under his touch and reached for her shirt hem to help him along faster.

"Easy." The word vibrated over her flesh, shooting sparks to all corners of her body.

"You're driving me" —she threw her head back as he flicked at her nipple with his tongue again— "crazy!"

Taking mercy on her, he drew her top up and over her head. When he skimmed his gaze over her body, she felt beautiful, safe and cherished. The sensation was something altogether new, and she was shocked to realize how amazing it felt to finally let down that guard. Until this moment, she'd never understood the true toll Antonio's disappearance had taken on her.

He popped the clasp of her bra and drew the strap over her shoulder in tiny increments that made her burn hotter. Need had her panties soaked, and she couldn't stop herself another minute—she went for his belt.

He lifted his head and flashed a look at her, piercing her with some unknown order she couldn't make out. But she lay there still, watching him push back onto his knees to work open his belt with sharp moves of his big hands. Then he popped the top button of his jeans, and she focused on that enticing bulge that snaked from the top of the zipper down the long line of his cargo pants.

She must have made some noise, because his eyes darkened with a dangerous spark. But she wasn't frightened—only turned on.

"You're fucking beautiful, lying there all dewy and ready for me. Show me how you pinch your nipples."

Her lips popped open in surprise. Nobody had ever asked such a thing of her before. But having this man give the order made her want to please him in all ways.

She raised her hands to her breasts and cupped them. He groaned, eyes lidding as he looked on.

Driven by his reaction, she closed her fingers over her distended nipples and squeezed lightly. He let out a hungry growl, and she moaned as excitement flipped low in her belly and pleasure shot through her nipples at her own touch.

"This is what you're made for, darlin'."

Pinching her nipples again, she watched his reaction to her and burned for more. She ran her hands down her torso and dipped one into her leggings and wet panties.

"Hell," he ground out. He let her stroke the folds of her slick pussy a moment before easing her hand out and raising it to his lips. As he darted his tongue over her fingers, he held her gaze prisoner.

"Nash… please. I need you to make me come."

He stuck her finger into his mouth and sucked. She almost came undone there and then. Her eyes slipped shut. When she opened them again, he was poised between her legs.

Watching a man like Nash undress her was one of the most thrilling experiences of her life, and she would relive it over and over again. The way his rough fingers worked down her leggings, pulled her panties off her ankles and discarded them… God, she was going to explode.

Then he fixed that dark gaze of his on her and parted her thighs. A bead of wetness slipped from her pussy even before he touched her. He ran a finger over the seam of her outer lips, making her moan and shake. But when he thumbed her apart and lowered his tongue to her needy bud, she cried out.

"Fucking heaven." He sank his tongue deep, cradling her ass and lifting her to feast on her pussy. Each rotation of his tongue on her clit had her splitting apart more, and soon she'd be nothing but a moaning, panting, trembling mess.

Uncaring, she slid her hand around his nape and clasped his face to her pussy. He sucked at her seam and drew one of her lips into his mouth. The brand new sensation rocketed her higher.

He released her and went for her clit. When he sucked that onto his tongue, she crested on a high wave of ecstasy and then came down hard. She orgasmed with a muffled scream, riding his tongue as shocks hit her system over and over again.

As she released a harsh breath, he buried his tongue into her opening and licked her juices out of her with long swipes. She clamped her fingers in his hair and held him right where she wanted him.

He raised his mouth, wet from her folds, and grated out, "You want to keep me down here eating your pussy, don't you, darlin'?"

His dirty talk had her on edge all over again.

It also made her feel powerful.

The sensation was new and completely unexpected. How could a sex act with a near stranger give her what she'd battled to achieve for a decade?

She wanted to feel strong and empowered, and Nash was giving her that just by setting her free.

"Say it." His demand was a rough stroke dragged over her senses.

Her stomach fluttered with a thousand butterflies as she stared into his eyes. "Eat my pussy till I come again."

* * * * *

Looking at this woman was enough to make a man feel a thousand feet tall. But watching her come apart for him had him feeling like a goddamn hero.

She was off-limits.

But she tasted so damn good.

He drove his tongue into her pussy again and pressed down on her clit with his thumb. She bucked upward, and he felt her clench around him, grabbing for more. She fucking deserved every screaming orgasm he could give her in the short time they had together.

Just knowing he'd have to walk away and leave her soon made him want to hurl some bullets, but he pushed the thought from his head and concentrated on pleasuring Nevaeh.

The soft little cries breaking from her plump lips had his cock like the hardest oak. It pushed against his fly, torturing him further with the pressure. Hell, he was splitting balls here, but he wasn't sinking into that tight body of hers until she'd come on his tongue a second time.

Clamping his fingers on her hips, he dragged her up to his lips. Mouthing her gently now, teasing his way up and down her soaking sex as she ground her hips in demand.

Fucking yesssss. Take all you want.

Realizing he'd let her make a slave of him if she begged him to was something he'd come to terms with later. He'd never wanted to please any woman this way, and that fucking scared him.

Deal with it later, Nash. Just like everything else.

He closed his lips lightly over her clit and nibbled.

Her fingers tightened on his hair, and he felt her muscles coil. Using his tongue along with his lips, he drove her on ruthlessly.

Come for me, he chanted in his head. When he slid two fingers inside her clenching heat, she gave a hard pulsation around his hand. Then another.

As she came apart in a squirming orgasm, total satisfaction spread across his face in the form of a smile. Her flavors swirled in his head, arousing the hell out of him. And he was motherfucking ready to take her — now.

Pressing his fingers into her deeper, he raised his head to watch her face. Euphoria had her features lit like an angel's, and she was — somehow — more fucking stunning. How the hell could that even be possible?

"Nash, I want you."

Keeping his fingers buried inside her, he looked into her eyes. "I'm big. Can you take me this deep?"

She nodded. He drove his fingers higher, deeper. "This deep?"

"Yes! Oh God. Please, Nash."

He lifted her a bit on his fingers, and her round ass hovered off the mattress. "You want to feel me this deep?"

Her eyes rolled back in her head.

That was all he could take. Drawing his fingers out of her, he went for his fly, attacking his clothes like it was his goddamn mission in life.

He could still walk away from this—there was still time. Keeping her safe was his top priority, and his duties to Ranger Ops and this mission were fucking real as hell right this minute.

But he was inches away from having everything he wanted.

Take her, his body urged. His cock throbbed, and his balls grew fuller.

He gripped his cock at the root and squeezed back the impending explosion.

"I don't have a condom," he ground out.

She shook her head. "I'm on birth control and I haven't had sex in a year."

"Dammit." Why couldn't she have told him anything but that?

"I'm checked regularly," he heard himself say as he shoved his cargos and boxers down his hips. His boots followed and the entire mass ended up on the floor.

Watching him, she wet her lips again, nearly shredding his control. When she slowly parted her thighs in invitation, giving him a glimpse of her gorgeous, wet pussy, he snapped.

Grabbing her by the hips, he dragged her over the mattress and up to meet his cock. With the purple head poised at the center of her, he looked into her eyes. "I swear to keep you safe, always."

In one plunge, he joined with her. The sensation was so fucking sweet it made his teeth ache, and damn if she didn't give the softest of cries that turned his heart inside out too.

Shaking from the effort of withholding from taking her like a rutting beast, he leaned in and captured her lips. The kiss was a smooth melding of lips coupled with an emotion he'd never known in his entire life.

God, she had his heart doing maneuvers he couldn't fathom or follow, and when she pulled him down so his weight was atop her, it suddenly became so much more than a physical need for him.

Shit. It was like... lovemaking.

He swept his tongue across hers and began to move. In slow, rhythmic pulses of his hips, he sank into her hot sheath and withdrew with a slowness that belied his lack of control. He wanted to make this good, because he had one goddamn shot at it.

Her fingers in his hair gave him some powerful electrical feelings in the vicinity of his heart. And his balls ached to blow.

He sank into her harder this time. She cried out, and he swallowed it on his kiss.

When he withdrew, she followed him, and how could he resist that temptation? He drove into her hard. She angled her hips to accept him to the deepest point, and he growled out against his orgasm, which was far too close to the surface.

With another thrust and then another, he felt her begin to tighten, clamping around him with her inner muscles. A quiver shook her.

"Fuck, I can't stop it." He slammed his mouth over hers and kissed her as his release hit, so intense that he lost focus of anything but the stars behind his eyes and the sensation of her clenching heat encircling him as she too began to shake from her own orgasm.

His hips moved on their own, and he couldn't stop kissing her if he tried. The taste was too sweet and real to walk away from.

Hell, he was in so much fucking trouble here.

With the round globe of her ass still cradled on his palm, he leaned back to stare into her eyes. He didn't know what to expect to see, but it sure as hell wasn't the look she was giving him, one of pure and utter joy and peace.

Releasing a grunt, he dropped his forehead to hers and breathed in her scent, a light breezy note of perfume like the ocean itself. Made sense, because she *was* like a siren, having risen up and tormented him right to the deepest possible depths.

"I have to move you, Nevaeh. Now."

She nodded against him, but it was more of a nuzzling against his skin.

Shit, he was sunk.

Chapter Five

"Sully, we got a domestic taking place right now." Woody's voice projected into Nash's ear as he drew his Sig from its holster.

"I hear it. Fuck. Guys, I think it's time to wrap up the reconnaissance and go in." He was already moving fast toward the side window. When he came across a plank of wood that looked to be from a half-demolished side porch, Cav and Jess joined up with him.

Cav grabbed one end of the board, and he and Nash shoved it hard through a window. Jess began to run up it and launched inside.

"I'm in. Room's empty. I'm gonna explore. They're screaming too loud—I don't think they heard that window break."

"Jesus. Cav, get in there and watch his six." Nash waved toward the window and Cavanagh scaled the board too, vanishing through the broken glass. How the big man fit through such a small opening would puzzle any onlooker, but they were trained for this.

"Linc, Lennon, skirt the back and see if you can enter that way. Woody, follow them. I'm going in behind Cav and Jess." Nash stepped on the board. It sagged beneath his weight, but he moved with speed and stealth. When he landed on his boots inside the room, he spotted Cav's back as he edged around a door.

The room he stood in was empty with only a few items of furniture pushed up against the walls. Everything they knew about this place was there were no search warrants or arrest records for any of the men they'd seen coming and going. To the public, they looked perfectly normal, but Jess had gotten one hell of a lead the previous night after using Nevaeh's code to slip in and hack one of their emails. That had opened a whole world of codes to crack, and Jess and Penn had stayed up most of the night digging through it until they found what they wanted.

Ten years before, these same men had operated internet sites that Antonio had regularly visited. Or breached. Either way, Ranger Ops had enough to proceed.

Moving swiftly, Nash ducked through the door, following the sounds of the domestic.

A shot fired, and it wasn't the sound of a Ranger Ops' Sig or one of their rifles.

"Watch your asses," he ordered as he turned and reached a closed door. The screaming of a woman— no, two women—was deafening, but a man's shouting covered even that. He was in a rage, cussing the females in rapid Spanish.

He wasn't the only one in a rage.

Nash lifted a boot and kicked in the door.

The stench of sweat and unwashed bodies hit him full in the face, and he turned instinctively to the man. Two women huddled in a corner, clinging to each other. Jess and Cav stormed in behind Nash and got the women on their feet and dragged them from the room as Nash aimed at the man's chest at point-blank range.

"Who the hell are you?" the thug demanded in his native tongue.

"Drop your weapon." Nash's focus went to the pistol aimed at his forehead, but he wasn't sweating it—not yet. What this guy didn't know was Woody was moving around the back right now and had eyes on the man through the window.

"You drop yours!"

The guy's finger twitched on the trigger, and then the window exploded in a thousand shards as Woody took the shot. The man collapsed, and Nash rushed him, kicking the weapon out of his reach and jamming the barrel of his semi-auto into his gut.

He barely restrained himself from killing the man, but Lang perched on his shoulder, urging him to deal with him minus his temper. The guy would be better use to them if he was alive to speak.

"Jess, Cav, get those women to safety. Linc and Lennon, come get this asshole and bring some bungee cords." He turned to the window. "Thanks, Woody."

"House is all clear, Sully. They're the only ones in it. And there's not a trace of an electronic in this fucking place." Lennon's Southern drawl filled Nash's comms unit.

Ten minutes later, they had the victim stabilized with his bleeding staunched, and he was tied with bungee cords to a chair. Nash fired questions at him, and the others kept a close scope on the perimeter of the building in case any of his buddies returned.

Finally, Nash let out a breath. "They took everything and left, he says. Gave him the place to stay with his women, but they had an argument between them about who was sharing his bed tonight, and he ordered them both to come to his bed. That made the fighting worse, and he says he stopped it. Jesus, what scum. Okay, sweep the place one more time, and then we're moving out."

Woody met Nash's gaze. "You know where they moved, don't you?"

"Yep."

"I hope we're launching through windows again, because that was an adrenaline rush." Lennon grinned and turned for the door with his weapon at the ready.

Woody gestured to the man bungeed to the wooden chair. "What do we do with this piece of shit?"

"Anybody who'd shoot at a woman deserves to have his balls chopped off and fed to him. But I'm feeling generous today. We'll leave and call in an anonymous tip to the paramedics that a man's been shot."

Woody reached for his cell. "Want me to do that now?"

"Nah, we'll wait a couple hours till he's in a healthy amount of pain."

It was clear from the man's face he didn't follow their English, and Nash took perverse pleasure in that fact.

When they regrouped back at the hostel, the guys began packing up all the gear. Under cover of darkness, the computers and surveillance systems were hauled out in black bags, and Linc paid off the hostel owner with a stack of bills.

Nash was itching to call his brother, who was guarding Nevaeh, and get word that she was safe, but not yet. He had to get his men situated in another part of the city.

For the move through the streets, they split up. Nash had Woody on his three and he was damn glad for it as they scouted the area. Setting up so close to the people they were trying to nab for kidnapping Antonio Vincent was a huge risk, but Nash had complete confidence in his team.

His mind continued to dart back to Nevaeh. He needed to make that call to his brother soon. Thank God the man had shown up when he did—Ranger Ops needed his expertise, and if Nash was truthful with himself, he didn't trust anybody else to protect Nevaeh.

That tenderness for her rose up like a bright sun. Dammit, he was going to struggle after this was all said and done—he was in deeper than he'd ever been from a single encounter with a woman in his bed.

He wasn't exactly a playboy, but he got his fair share of sex. What he'd shared with Nevaeh was not simple wham-bam-thank-you-ma'am. That had him wondering how the hell to get out of the situation without leaving her feeling used and unworthy.

He pushed out a sigh.

"All right, man?" Woody paced next to him, their shoes squashing into the sandy soil that ran parallel to the property they were to inhabit as soon as the others slipped in.

"Yeah." He shot his buddy a look. They hadn't been working together all that long, but already Nash was feeling bonds with all his men, especially after the Sabine River incident. He grunted, and Woody looked to him.

"What is it?"

"Just thinkin'." Nash bit back a smile. "Wondered how long that asshole we shot is gonna be laid up with that bullet wound."

Woody snorted. "I don't know. It was a good meaty chunk taken out of his shoulder."

They shared a quiet chuckle. Then suddenly, the hairs on the back of Nash's neck went up.

Covertly, from the corner of his eye, he noted two men dogging them about fifty feet away.

Woody noted it too, but the only indication he gave was a tightening of his lips. He raised a hand and rubbed at his jaw. "I think we're made, man."

"I got that too. Thinkin' of an exit strategy versus confrontation."

"I got an idea."

"I'm all for it," Nash said.

Suddenly, Woody stopped and faced him. "Kiss me," he said.

Nash blinked. Before he could move, Woody leaned in, grabbed Nash by the nape and laid one square on his mouth.

He barely registered the odd sensation of kissing a man let alone his teammate, because he was too busy noting the posture of the two guys following them. They relaxed visibly and detoured in another direction.

Woody pulled back and swiped his mouth. "Gah. You ate the burritos, didn't you? You never did fucking say whether or not they make you gassy."

"Fuck you." He grinned as he shot a look back toward the men, who were now ignoring him and Woody, thinking them just a couple of amorous men out for a walk. He gave Woody a sideways glance. "Good ploy, but what the actual fuck was that?"

Woody laughed. "I just saved our asses."

"No. I meant the tongue."

He grinned. "That was for effect—we had to look legitimate to those guys or they'd be on to us." He smiled wider. "Or maybe it was just me being adventurous."

"Asshole." He shook his head. "If you ever try that again, I'll—"

"Get the lube?" Woody arched a brow.

They were laughing now. They hadn't taken two steps before Linc's voice entered their ears, loud and clear. "If you two are finished making out, you'd better hurry over here. We've got an issue."

* * * * *

Nevaeh sat near the window, though not close. Penn had instructed her to keep clear of the windows directly just in case.

In case of what? She didn't want to think about that answer. So she pushed it firmly from her head and sat with her legs curled under her, staring at the sleepy neighborhood. It was siesta, and she wasn't one for lying down and resting during the day, so she just watched the people go into their houses for an hour and enjoyed the silence in her own way.

So many times, she'd thought about taking Nash up on that offer to return home. She'd been in this house alone for three days now, with his brother Penn as bodyguard. The man took his job seriously, too, walking the house nonstop and checking windows and doors. At night, she had no idea if he slept, but each time she woke, she heard him walking the floors, on patrol.

He was coming now. She lifted her head and turned it toward the doorway just as the huge man filled the frame. She'd had plenty of time to study him, and she'd made a lot of familial connections between him and Nash. They were of the same height and while Nash's chest was broader, Penn's biceps were beefier. The two could do some major damage to anyone who crossed them. And she liked how Penn's eyes reminded her of the man she'd begged to make her come only a few nights ago.

"What is it?" she asked Penn.

"Nash is on his way. He'll be here in five."

Her heart shouldn't leap that way—why did it? So what if she'd taken her ease with the man and allowed him to break through her barricades. It wasn't more.

So why did her heart tell her otherwise?

She nodded and got up.

Penn started forward to put himself between her and the window, prepared to take a bullet for her on Nash's order.

Seeing Penn move, she inched to the side out of the way of the window just to keep him happy. Then she found herself moving to the nearest mirror to check her appearance.

Stupid. What had happened between her and the captain of the special ops team had been purely physical — and was unlikely to happen a second time. Hell, she still wasn't even sure he liked her. After all, a man didn't need to like a woman to sleep with her.

Penn's amused look sent her scurrying from the mirror. Luckily, he turned and left the space, leaving her alone with a burning face. She followed him to the door. When he opened it and Nash crowded inside, her heart gave another trembling leap.

He was bigger than she remembered. Wearing jeans and a black T-shirt, he couldn't look hotter. When he lifted his head and grazed his eyes over her, she felt the touch down to the core of her being.

She gulped too. He was sporting a bruised jaw, and a cut rode the edge of his cheekbone.

He turned his stare from her, leaving her feeling sweaty and breathless but also let down. She knew it — he didn't like her. She'd just made a fool of herself thinking there might be more to their connection.

He locked hands with Penn in a midair arm-wrestling match. "All good, bro?" Penn asked. "I know you got into some shit."

He gave a faint nod. "Deep shit. But we got through with only a few bumps and bruises."

"All good here." Penn tipped his head toward her, and if she hadn't been staring hard at Nash, she would have missed the way his eyes narrowed. Not that she understood it.

He looked to her again, and a slow warmth crept over her insides. If she looked at him much longer, she'd begin that burn, and then she'd probably hurl herself at him and beg him to take her again.

She had to keep some distance. Besides, she was here for Antonio, and Nash could have information on him.

"I got it for now. Take a break." Nash's low order to Penn worked its way under Nevaeh's skin, burrowing in places that sounds shouldn't affect.

"I'll be down at the pub if you need me." Penn opened the door, and without a backward glance, left.

Nash didn't budge from his spot in front of the door. He did lower the backpack he was carrying to the floor and reach behind himself and twist the lock, though. She shifted from foot to foot, feeling oddly turned on and totally nervous in front of this man. She hadn't seen him since that night. They hadn't talked about what they'd done, and she had no clue what had gone through his mind afterward. Maybe nothing—he could have just forgotten about it.

"You all right?" he asked, low.

She nodded, drawing her arms up to wrap around her middle. His gaze dipped over her breasts, pushed upward from her arms. She swallowed down another leap of excitement.

"Do you have any news on Antonio?"

He nodded and then motioned to the cheap sofa. It had been placed in the middle of the room, but Penn had pushed it up against a wall without windows. She felt like she had a hit out on her or

116

something, with all the protective measures he'd taken to keep her safe.

She moved to the sofa and sank into the corner, drawing her knees up.

He stood before her, staring down into her eyes for a moment. He pushed out a sigh. "Don't do that. Don't shield yourself from me."

Before she could guess his intentions, he sat and dragged her into his lap.

She fell still. This was how it had all begun the other night. With her seated across his steely-hard thighs and him offering up comfort during a difficult situation. One thing had led to another, and...

She gazed at his mouth, so hard and inviting. Yet she saw a new strain around his lips and corners of his eyes. Whatever had happened out there had affected him.

"What happened?" she asked softly.

He gave a light shake of his head. "Can't say much."

"Nash..."

He surprised her by cupping her cheek in his big palm and staring straight into her eyes. "Tell me you're all right."

"I am." She leaned into his touch, not knowing if she should be doing this. But she was so drawn to him, to his presence, his touch, even the way he looked at her. It was like she was his marionette, and he had hold of all her strings.

"Penn was good to you?"

"Of course. I figured you wouldn't have left him to watch over me if you had any doubts."

A trace of a smile touched his lips but never fully materialized. "I brought you some things, books and magazines, to help pass the time."

She had to ask. "What about Antonio?"

"He's alive."

The words punched the breath right out of her. She hung forward, panting to gain air. Nash drew her against his chest for support, and she leaned against him hard. Her mind battled with doubts — he could be wrong. Others had been over the years. The cops or Texas Rangers would show up asking questions again, and she and her parents knew something had tipped them off or they'd found some clue. But all had been dead-ends.

Nash had spotted him, though.

Nash smoothed a hand down her spine. "I know you're probably shocked to hear it, but I confirmed it myself. Antonio is alive, and we know how to get him. We're just waiting for the opportunity."

"Then..." She could hardly speak, she felt so shaky. "My password helped in some way? It led you to the him somehow? What happened?"

"I can't fill you in on everything right now. It's classified information, and I'm not at leave to discuss it even with you. I'm sorry about that. But I saw him myself, with my own eyes. He's alive and has been forced into service by some men who deal in a lot of illegal online activity. Your brother hacked them ten years ago, and that put him on their radar. They lured him down here to discuss a partnership that would set him and his family members up for life — then they nabbed him and now he's a slave for them, pure and simple."

She pushed back to stare at Nash. His jaw worked as though he was grinding his teeth, and the warmth in his eyes was replaced by a cold, hard expression she didn't want to meet in a dark alley.

"Is he harmed?"

"Not outwardly, no."

She didn't want to think about the toll such a life the past decade had taken on Antonio. But he was alive! They'd deal with everything else later.

"My parents will be so happy! Oh my God, I need to contact them."

He held her in place, locking her to his lap before she could move off. "You can't do that, Nevaeh. We have to take our time with this and do things in order. We can't risk your brother's life, and it was bad enough those guys—" He broke off, lips pressed together, sealing in anything more he was about to say.

She made an involuntary noise in her throat that had his eyes clearing and his gaze riveted on hers once more.

"I promise I will get him outta there, Nevaeh."

"I know you will. If anyone can, it's you and your men. You've gotten so much further than anybody yet."

He didn't respond to her statement but brushed a tendril of her loose hair behind her ear, raising a shiver in her. "Tell me what you've been doing the past few days."

She fumbled to find anything to say besides dwelling on everything that could go wrong. That she'd go home without a brother again... or never see Nash again.

"Not much. Eating. It seems like Penn feels he needs to bring me a lot of food."

He chuckled. "Probably because he eats nonstop and always has. As kids, our mother found out he was eating some of my portions too. He was always bigger than me, even though he was younger. Then I hit my growth spurt and evened things out."

A smile touched her lips, thinking of Nash as a child and hearing about his past. He was letting her in, if even a little bit. And surely he wouldn't do that with just anybody. He trusted her enough to share this story.

"Brothers can be a pain," she said, swallowing hard.

"They can." He cradled her cheek again, this time breathing harder. She struggled with the urge to lean forward and press her lips against his, to feel his hardness again and know the complete abandon of letting go.

"Hell…" The word came off his lips as a puff of air.

"Nash, we didn't discuss what happened between us."

He locked his gaze onto her mouth. She squirmed closer to him.

When he swooped in and captured her lips, she gasped out. He crushed her to his chest, and she wrapped her arms around his broad shoulders as he plundered her without hesitation, without apology.

She burned for more, kissing him back with everything in her. When he laid her back on the couch and worked his hand under her top to cup her breast, she gave a cry. This passion, lust or whatever it was between them was too strong for her to deny, and she didn't want to be alone anymore.

She towed him down atop her, loving the feel of his weight and the way his shoulders sheltered her so perfectly. When he breached her bra and began to toy with her nipples, she strained upward.

Leaning on one shoulder, he freed both hands and plunged one into her shorts. Her panties were already damp, and she flooded with desire at the first touch of his callused fingers.

Reaching down, she popped the button and slid down the zipper to give him better access, and he doubled his kiss, tormenting her with each pass of his tongue through her mouth.

One fingertip rested against her clit. She bucked upward to get closer to it. He pressed down, applying the scantest touch that was driving her crazy.

"I've never needed anybody this way," she rasped.

His eyes were darker than ever. His eyelids slipped downward to cover the blazing depths. "Ask me to touch this sweet pussy."

"Yes! Nash, touch me."

Without hesitation, he circled her stiff nubbin. Electric pleasure rushed through her. Her hips moved by themselves, and he continued to drive her upward toward an unseen pinnacle, hard and fast.

She clung to him, found his lips. The moment stretched on, and her body grew tauter. When she started to shake from the force of the orgasm coming her way, he raised his head and stared into her eyes.

"Come for me. Now."

The command was too much. She gave in, floating on air as he continued to strum her clit through the waves of her release. She curled toward him, and he eased his arm under her spine to draw her even closer. The silence filling the air was charged with so many unspoken words, yet she didn't know how to tell him how he made her feel just now.

She'd just have to show him.

She reached for his fly, but he drew his fingers from her shorts and stopped her.

"Nevaeh."

"Yes?"

"I can't compromise you further. I've already done enough damage."

He pulled back and stood, leaving her feeling more confused about how to take back her life, to take what she wanted, than ever.

* * * * *

Damage—that fucking word didn't begin to cover it. Why the hell had he given up all control and touched her? Just laying hands on her did unspeakable things to his insides, and it didn't have to do with his need to get off, either.

When she gave him that look, how could he resist?

He couldn't.

He *hadn't*—twice now.

Maybe it was the shit he'd had to do back there on the outskirts of the city in order to protect the Ranger Ops' position. He'd also done it for Antonio Vincent, and that had a lot to do with Nevaeh too.

Find Antonio, make Nevaeh happy.

Only it wasn't his damn job to make people happy, only stop crime, find justice. Things had gotten goddamn complicated, though.

He stepped into the kitchen. Bringing his fingers to his nose to catch her feminine scent was his first mistake. Or his second or third, who the hell knew by this time? He was wrecked, his cock throbbing with the demand to go back there, gather that beautiful woman into his arms and find the closest bed.

Locating the bathroom, he washed his hands and forced his dick back into a more comfortable position in his jeans. The need was real, but he couldn't let it control him.

He also felt like a fucking jerk for walking away from Nevaeh like that. When he returned to the living room, she was nowhere to be seen, so he had to explore the house until he found a closed door.

Rapping softly, he said, "Nevaeh?"

She didn't reply. Shit, what now?

"Nevaeh, darlin', open up. We need to talk."

No response.

He listened hard at the door but didn't hear a noise inside. His mind kicked into high gear, propelling him toward a conclusion that she was inside that room, in trouble. Maybe someone had sneaked inside and taken her hostage while he was washing her delicious juices off his hands to keep himself from licking his fingers clean.

"Nevaeh!"

No answer. *That does it.*

Shoving hard with his shoulder, he busted the door inward. She whirled at his forced entry, eyes wide and jaw dropped.

"What the hell are you doing?" she demanded.

He scanned her body and their surroundings, but she was safe. No intruder, just his overactive mind at work.

"You didn't answer the door."

"Because I didn't feel like talking to you, Nash. You broke the lock and handle!"

"I had to make certain you were safe."

"Safe? What would I be doing?"

He pinched the bridge of his nose. Things were getting out of control, and fast. He had to get hold of himself and the situation.

"Look, I want to talk to you. What just happened—"

"Was nothing."

Fuck, that hurt. It shouldn't, but it did. He also deserved it.

But he couldn't let things drop this way. He wasn't an asshole.

He stepped forward and took her by the shoulders. Holding her in place, he stared into her eyes. "Nevaeh, I've already broken about a hundred rules just by touching you. Christ, it's not that I don't want to. But I have to stay focused, to find your brother."

"I know," she said in a hollow way. "I thought of it after you left days ago, that we couldn't let anything happen between us again. Then I saw you, and I guess I went a little crazy."

Damn, that made him feel like a king, and he didn't deserve it. His grip on her shoulders turned into a caress. He kneaded at the tense knots in her shoulders. "You're a strong and special woman."

She sighed. "I can't be anything but strong. I had to be here for my parents all these years. As soon as they'd begin their lives again, it seemed a short time later some Texas Ranger would show up asking questions, and then they'd sink back into that same old despair. Their grief never had resolution, and how could it when they were constantly being reminded of their son being missing? I had to hold them together more often than not."

"And you're amazing because of that. Many daughters might have run to escape it or turned to substance abuse. You've shown what you're made of."

She eyed him. "What are you getting at, Nash?"

He laughed, an unexpected sound in the quiet of the house. "See? Smart too."

"Now I know you're trying to get me to do something. What is it? Because if you want me to go back to Texas now, you're about to see just how strong I am."

Smoothing his hands down her arms, he shook his head. "You have a radar, don't you? Ever considered the Texas Rangers?"

Her expression softened. "No. Now tell me what it is."

He steered her to sit down on the bed and sank next to her, close but not touching. It was difficult to think with the silky feel of her under his hands, and he couldn't risk not getting this question across.

"A few days back we came across some women who we'd rescued from a man who was terrorizing them. It was clear they're in the skin trade, but that's no reason. We got them to safety, questioned them and let them go. But when we ran across them again, we found them drugged out of their minds and back in it. Not surprising."

She twisted her fingers together, listening.

Nash went on, "One said something that had my guy on alert, and he was listening close. He took them into custody and kept them until the shit was out of their systems and they could answer our questions. They offered some information about the habits of the men who nabbed Antonio, and from there, we began scouting local hangouts and bars. We approached the cops about it, but that's a fucking dead end. Those guys don't give a damn about our problem. Anyway..."

He took her hands to stop the twisting action, gently untwining her fingers and clasping them in his own. She relaxed a bit, and he continued.

"We were frustrated at this point and about to switch to another approach, when I found a kid who steered us to an old lady."

"An old lady? Is she someone's mother or something?"

"No. She's a woman who lives on an upper floor of a building near one of theirs. While she sits on her landing, looking harmless, she sees things."

"And she knows where Antonio is?" Hope was written over her face.

"Not exactly. And she wasn't one to talk freely either. Clearly, she'd lived long enough to know whether or not to spill information."

"But she did talk." Nevaeh clutched his hand, her statement forceful as if she was trying to make it so because she wanted it so badly.

He nodded. "She gave us some information, yes. But in trade."

"Trade. Money?"

"No. She has enough of that, but what she needed was help."

"What kind of help? Are those men terrorizing her too?"

"No, this is something totally different. First, she pulled us into her house, all six of us, and insisted on feeding us. Total strangers to her, but she didn't care."

"Oh, an *abuela* for sure."

128

He nodded at the mention of grandmother. "Yes, and great food too. Anyway, when we were finished eating, she asked us to do some things for her around her place. Her door handle wasn't working in one room and a window wasn't opening in another."

Nevaeh's eyes popped in surprise. "She needed handymen?"

"Seems so. She has family, of course, but says they're busy working too much. Said that's the trouble with young people, never slowing down to live. Anyhow, I digress. She asked for something else."

"Okay," she drawled out, suspecting Nash was coming to a conclusion.

"She wants to throw her granddaughter a huge *Quincinera* party, but she doesn't have the help."

"Shit. This is where you offered for me to go help, isn't it?"

"See? I said you were smart."

She jumped off the bed and took two steps, folding her arms across her chest. Hell, even when she scowled, she looked beautiful. "I'm supposed to go help this old woman prepare for a party?"

He stood and took her by the hands again. "Look, there's no lowly task in a team. We need you, Nevaeh. We don't have time for this, but she gave us information that was very helpful, and it's a repayment. Besides, she might think of something else that could help, and you would be in a position to talk to her in a relaxed atmosphere."

"So while we chop peppers and onions, we talk about what crimes the jerks across the street are committing?"

"Something like that, yeah. Look, I won't force you into doing this, but I'm asking. Besides, she really is nice and could use some help. You'd be safe with her, and I'll have Penn posted outside the building to watch over you both."

"Damn. How am I supposed to say no to this? I want to do anything I can to find Antonio and get him back. I'm closer than I've ever been since the day he disappeared. So yes, of course, I'll do it. But I have to confess I'm not very good at talking to people. I'm too quiet and awkward."

"You talk to me easily. You'll be fine. It's settled. Now gather your things." He didn't add: *Before I kiss you and we never leave this room.* But it was all he could think.

Chapter Six

How had Nevaeh gotten herself into this situation? She was a simple bookkeeper, a good daughter and her favorite thing was catching a Saturday matinee alone. Now she was standing in a strange woman's kitchen, spit-shining every surface to the woman's strict instructions.

It seemed the family didn't often come to visit the dear old woman with the charming name of Altagracia. She was old-school to the core, set in the ways she did things, even scrubbing the kitchen.

As she worked, Nevaeh listened to Altagracia's broken English interspersed with Spanish here and there when her English failed her. The entire first day was spent cleaning the kitchen until every pot and surface gleamed. By then Nevaeh had listened to tales of all the woman's seven children who were scattered throughout Mexico and her sixteen grandchildren, the youngest of which was turning fifteen soon and would receive a special gift of her grandmother's party.

"It's the last chance I have to spoil one of the babies before she grows up and leaves to have babies of her own." Altagracia drew a handkerchief to her eyes, dabbing at a tear.

"Well, I'm sure she will appreciate the party so much. Your home is beautiful, but it's small. Will it fit everyone who's coming?" Nevaeh's question sent the woman off into a tizzy about moving furniture back against walls in order to gain more floor space. That led Nevaeh on a whirlwind trip through the house, inspecting furniture and seeing how much more needed to be done in order to make Altagracia happy.

Strange, but even after only a day of knowing the woman, Nevaeh felt as if she'd gained a new friend. They hadn't yet gotten to a conversation involving the things Altagracia saw from her upper landing where she spent so much time looking out over the neighborhood, but Nevaeh was certain it would come. Surely, the old lady would run out of stories about her family.

Before Nevaeh dropped into the bed she was given to sleep in, she pulled aside the heavy, dusty drapery to see a man standing in the shadows below. Penn.

She lifted her gaze to the city beyond and the buildings in shades of yellow or clay, many aged and needing repairs on walls or roofs. Somewhere out there was her brother. And also Nash.

It was impossible not to linger over thoughts of the rugged special ops captain. Just knowing him lent to the strangeness of her current situation. This felt as far from her life as she could ever imagine. A month ago, if someone had suggested she'd be in Mexico and lusting after a man like Nash, she would have giggled and scoffed it off.

She pressed a palm over her stomach, low where it fluttered with arousal. Did she have to be so attracted to Nash? He was handsome but in a way that grew on her the more she looked at him.

He seemed to break through many of her barriers too—which she'd never realized she needed let alone wanted. But fact was, she had been so strong for so many years that she didn't know how to shed her armor anymore. Nash had sensed it and stripped it away from her with a single touch, and now she wanted to melt into his arms every day.

She shook herself. This wasn't permanent. Sure, he'd shown her a new way of living, but she would be taking this knowledge and moving on from here alone. After this was all over—one way or another—she'd return to Texas and try to employ all the things she'd learned on this trip. Maybe in time she'd find another man, though she couldn't guess who could stand up to Nash's standard.

A light rap on her door had her scuttling from the window to open it. Altagracia stood there in her nightgown, shadows dipping into the creases of her face. "Everything comfortable, my dear?" the old woman asked, and Nevaeh once again realized how lonesome she must be here rattling around the house all day thinking of her family she missed.

Reaching out, Nevaeh touched her arm. It felt thin but wiry, like a bird's. A strong old bird, flitting from one thing to another and sometimes landing to watch over the city. The notion brought a smile to Nevaeh's lips.

"Quite comfortable, thank you. Do you need anything? I could fetch you a drink if you need it," Nevaeh offered.

"Oh no, no. Thank you. Tomorrow, we'd best start on the dining room. We don't have much time."

Nevaeh patted her arm. "No, we don't." Her words rang true—their paths would cross for a very brief time. It was unlikely she'd ever see Altagracia again, and she really did enjoy this time with the woman. Simply working to make someone else happy made Nevaeh happy too, and that was unexpected.

"I'll get up at dawn to begin," she assured her.

* * * * *

Nash checked his ammunition and pocketed another handful into a cargo pocket on his vest. Then he withdrew his knife and checked the edge against his forearm, shaving off a patch of hair. Satisfied it was sharp enough to gut a whale, he returned it to its hidden spot strapped to his calf and continued on.

Halfway through testing his backup pistol, he looked up to find his brother in the doorway.

"What're you doing here?" Nash asked.

"Comin' to see if there's anything I can do for you."

Nash arched a brow. "And if there isn't?"

134

"Then I head on down the road to the next person in need."

"Funny how you popped up here in Mexico when we arrived." It wasn't coincidence at all that Penn had shown up when they needed him most. That seventh man had really made a world of difference in so many ways. It also meant Nash could focus on what he needed to do as captain. Since he was winging much of it, he needed to center his concentration on the mission.

Penn had rallied a few hundred feet from Altagracia's home, and they could still keep watch on the entrances while they worked out their plan. Penn gave Nash a shit-eating grin. "Yeah, funny how that worked out."

Nash checked more of his gear, messing with his comms unit that had been cutting out on occasion. He needed to have Jess, who was best with anything electronic, have a look at it.

He tucked it away for later inspection and looked up at Penn. "There might be something you could do for me."

Penn leaned against the wall and crossed his arms in a casual manner. "Watch over your girl?"

Nash's heart did a tuck-and-roll, tumbling end over end for a breathless moment. When he recovered, he said, "She's not my girl."

Penn grunted.

"What's that for?" Nash wasn't exactly pissed, but he was irritated. Last thing he needed was his kid brother teasing him about his very forbidden—but very real—connection to Nevaeh.

"You can't fool me. The others, maybe. They don't know you as well as I do. But Nevaeh has a look about her when you're not around."

Nash's mind zapped to the point. "What look?"

"The look a well-loved woman does when she's waiting to be loved again."

He opened his mouth to respond to that with a denial, but suddenly the guys filed into the room.

Penn let the topic drop, thank God, and Nash was able to take charge. "All right, guys, I hope you've checked all your gear. We can't fuck up a single thing tonight." He reached into his pocket and extracted the comms unit. He handed it to Jess. "Having some trouble with this cutting out. See what you can do."

"On it, captain." Jess didn't look up from the small device on his palm and sank to a chair to mess with it.

"All right, what we've got is a third generation dirtbag named Martin Lopez. Grandfather was arrested in the sixties on weapons smuggling. He did thirty years and died in prison. His father was cartel in the eighties, retired and handed over his business to his son, who saw it was a risky way of playing and wised up. He got out and found a more lucrative business in swindling people out of money but soon turned to theft via the internet, which Antonio has played a major role in over the past decade. Thanks to Jess and Linc for their deep digging skills to discover all this." He looked to the men, who gave him sharp nods.

Nash continued, "We all know the plan. The map's scorched on your brains too."

They all nodded.

"We get in, scope the place for Vincent, and get the fuck out. We only fire our weapons if there is a threat, and then we shoot to kill. We can't leave anybody lingering with vengeance on their minds after this. Got it?"

The clandestine mission in the wee hours of the night was a solidly thought-out plan, yet shit could always go sideways.

Nash looked from man to man, each as skilled and hardened in tactical training and counterterrorism. If anybody could get in that building, find their mark and slip out without too much bloodshed, it was them.

"We may be new to this game, men, but even the Knight brothers started somewhere." Nash held out his fist, and five others dropped into the center of their circle, bumping knuckles. "Guts and glory one mission at a time, right?"

Penn chuckled. "Man, are you seriously gonna steal Knight Ops' motto now?"

Nash looked up at his brother standing on the outside of their circle and straightened. "Brother, you deserve to be standing here right now. Life dealt you a bum hand, but you have made the most of it and continued with what you're passionate about. If that isn't guts and glory, I don't know what the fuck is."

His brother dropped his gaze, and Nash knew it was because he was overcome with emotion at Nash's praise. Cavanagh walked up to Penn and punched him on the shoulder. "Dude."

Penn took a swing as if he was going to punch Cavanagh, but instead he clasped hands with the man. The others moved up to Penn to do the same, an offer of respect. Then Nash gave his brother a hug. Penn brought his arms around him in a hard embrace that would have made their momma tear up.

"You know the plan," Nash told him.

"Yup. Get her out whether or not you rescue Vincent."

"That's right." Nash stepped back.

Penn eyed him. "Don't forget what I said about a well-loved woman. Who knows how long she'll wait." With that, he gave Nash a salute and headed for the door.

Nash didn't watch him go—only God knew when he'd see his brother again, but Penn always had a way of turning up when most needed. Turning toward his men, Nash met their gazes. "Time to do this thing."

* * * * *

"Spread out. Get in your positions." Nash's order even had him on high alert, his senses pinging around the perimeter of the building they were about to invade. Going back three generations had given them the exact location of Lopez, and they'd had eyes on this place for two days now. Antonio Vincent was definitely inside.

Whether or not the man wanted to be rescued was another thing. They were about to find out.

He shot a look toward the corner, but Woody wasn't moving. Why wasn't he moving?

"I said spread out, goddammit!"

His second on the team didn't budge from his position. It took Nash all of two seconds to understand what was happening—his comms unit still wasn't fucking working. Of all the times.

He made a sound with his boot on the ground that had Woody turning his way. Nash pointed to his ear and shook his head to indicate he didn't have communication. Woody's lips hardened, and then they moved slightly as he informed his other teammates.

Shit. Nash was cut off from the others, but he still had to lead them. There was only one way to go about it.

Lifting a hand, he gestured. Woody gave a nod and spoke to the others. Hell, it wasn't ideal, but it had worked, and Nash was certain he could still keep his guys safe and raining hell on this place with or without a way to tell them.

A noise from inside had him straining to hear. Leaning forward, he listened hard even as he held up a hand to his ear for Woody to see. Nash indicated he could hear somebody talking inside.

That meant not all were asleep despite the hour. They'd expected as much—Lopez wasn't stupid enough to leave his headquarters unguarded. By Ranger Ops' educated guess, there were at least three men guarding this place. The one on the roof was their first target to take down. Jess had asked for that job specifically, saying he was good at sneaking up on people and a good knock over the head could incapacitate him while they got in and got out again.

Nash's heart thumped as he made out a spotty word here and there. Fuck—the guys inside were talking about moving the operation. That could mean they'd all be awake and on the go, in positions Ranger Ops hadn't expected.

Woody was looking to Nash when he relayed this by using a series of hand gestures. Hell, he hoped his teammate got all that. For all he knew, Woody had just told the team to disburse and go grab a bucket of chicken.

He tried his comms device one more time, but it was clear he wasn't engaged. No time to lament the fact now—he had to use what resources he had, and that was his wits.

A few seconds later, the talking inside the building droned off.

He looked to Woody. *Time to move.*

Now *that* Woody got. He nodded and headed off, running in a crouch. Nash rounded the corner and set eyes on Cavanagh. He pointed up at the roof, and Nash nodded. Jess had done his job — there were only two other guards to take down.

Time seemed to pass in a blink, and Nash was damn proud of his men, who'd managed to make all the right moves even without their captain's direct communication. They converged on a back door, and Nash gestured to take it out.

Inside, they followed the sound of voices. Lennon, nearest to Nash, gave a series of hand gestures, telling him what he thought they should do.

Take them all, get Vincent and go.

Nash gestured back. *Get eyes in that room and find out if Vincent is among them.*

Lennon gave a nod, and then they were splitting off again, Jess providing the surveillance they needed by way of a tiny camera aimed under the crack in the door. Jess turned to them and gave a head shake.

He wasn't inside.

Minutes later, they were separated again, Nash communicating with whoever was nearest and relying on them to convey the commands to the others. But since they were trying to remain as silent

141

as possible, the hand signals were more efficient anyhow.

By now, Penn would have Nevaeh well on the way to the border—he wouldn't have wasted any time getting her out. One method or another, they were ending this today. Enough fucking around. Nash wasn't a man to sit and twiddle his thumbs, and all the surveillance and posing as drunk tourists had tried his patience. It was time for action.

Gun raised against any threat he might encounter, he threw out his sense of hearing into the house. A low hum met his ears—to the right. He turned and followed it. Jess stood just outside a door, listening too. He and Nash exchanged a few signals, and Nash's adrenaline spiked.

He was inside. Vincent was right within reach.

Nash gestured that they were going to subdue the man and then drag him out. If they didn't silence him first, Vincent was sure to raise an alarm and bring all the firepower of the household down on Ranger Ops.

Nash held up three fingers. Jess gave a nod, counting down with him. Then they burst into the room.

* * * * *

When Nash first spoke in English to Antonio Vincent, the man stared at him as though he didn't understand his first language. Then his eyes cleared, and he nodded.

142

"Come with us. We're here to get you home." Nash could already see the hesitation creeping over Vincent's face. Fuck, what if he wouldn't leave? Over a decade, he would have formed some sick version of a brotherhood with these men who had first been his captors.

Seeing he was about to refuse to leave with them, Nash added, "I have your sister waiting for you."

"Nevaeh." The name came off his lips as a rough, gritty series of syllables. And no wonder. He probably hadn't spoken her name aloud in ten years.

The name effected Nash as well, but he wasn't acknowledging that right now. He nodded and pointed to the door.

For a moment, Vincent didn't follow him. Jess waved at Nash, indicating they were running out of time.

Nash looked to Vincent. "Your call. Live in slavery with these guys forever or come home and take up your life again. Make the choice, man."

Vincent stood. Now that Nash was up close to him, he saw that outwardly, he was changed from the photo of the youthful man he'd been. He was in his thirties now, a lifetime behind him.

But a lifetime ahead of him too, if he chose to take it.

Jess was losing his shit in the doorway, and Nash knew time was not on their side. He pointed to the door and surged forward, through it. Whether or not Vincent would follow was on him.

Cavanagh appeared from around a corner. Suddenly, he jerked his weapon upward, at someone standing behind Nash.

He lurched to the side even as he knew who it was — Vincent had decided to come after all.

Cavanagh lowered his weapon and the three of them, along with Vincent, made a break for it. A heavy thud sounded from their left, and Nash started off that way, waving for the other two to get Vincent to safety.

With his weapon raised, Nash hurried toward the noise. Just then Woody appeared and then a pair of boots, followed by the legs of a man he was dragging out.

Nash jolted to a halt as he saw what had happened — during some hand-to-hand combat, Linc had been knocked unconscious. A glance back into the room showed Nash that the curtains were up in flames and a man lay face down in a pool of blood.

Fuck! Nash made a grab for Linc's shoulders, and between him and Woody, they heaved him up and over Nash's shoulder. Shit, the guy weighed a ton, but Nash couldn't move slowly. That fire would bring everyone running their way in a hurry.

Woody cleared the path, head swinging left and right as they converged on the exit. The others were out, including Vincent. Nash could feel Linc stirring and grabbed the back of his thigh to keep him still. Then Woody launched out the back door with Nash and Linc right on his tail.

A shot exploded by Nash's head — and another as Woody spun, aimed and fired.

The man crumpled, jaw skidding across the sparse grass of the yard.

Another man appeared, and Nash's fury rose up, hot and bright. That motherfucker he'd bungeed to a chair and left wounded was on his feet and had his sights on them.

So much for keeping his anger in check. *It didn't help in this case, Lang, you old son of a bitch.*

"Get the fuck outta here," Nash ordered, firing off a shot as he booked it. Something darted by his peripheral vision, and he choked off a cuss.

He didn't want to say what he'd seen — it was exactly what he had feared.

They hoofed it fast, with Woody hurling bullets through the night and Cavanaugh backing him up. Over Nash's shoulder, Linc groaned. "I got ya, man. Hold on," Nash ground out.

Lennon made it to the vehicle first, throwing open a door. The men piled in, and Jess jumped behind the wheel. Cavanagh helped Nash get Linc inside, and Nash slammed the door, yelling, "Drive!" though his instinct was to go back and level the fucking place.

A glance back showed him the house was up in flames, one corner engulfed and fire shooting from a window that had exploded outward.

Lennon looked around the vehicle. "Where the fuck's Vincent?"

Jess slammed on the brakes, and they looked at each other.

"I saw him take off back to the house. He doesn't want to be rescued. Goddammit!" Nash punched the seat in front of him.

"Holy hell, I didn't expect this," Jess said quietly.

"Drive!" Nash demanded.

As they pealed through the streets, his chest burned with more anger than he'd felt in a long fucking time.

How was he going to break the news to Nevaeh that her brother had chosen to turn back?

Chapter Seven

Nevaeh stared at the gray wall of her cubicle. Nothing added up. It had been a week since she'd come back from Mexico—a week since Ranger Ops had gone in after Antonio—and still no word.

In some circles, no news was good news, but she couldn't image that was the case here.

Thankfully she hadn't told her parents where she was headed, and that protected them now. She couldn't imagine getting their hopes up only to dash them away. They'd suffered enough heartbreak over the years.

Her vision blurred. She blinked and the gray wall came back into focus.

When Penn had put her on the plane back to Texas, he'd assured her everything would be all right. But he'd lied, hadn't he? Something had gone horribly wrong, and they hadn't found her brother.

Or it was something worse.

She didn't want to think on that too long, so she turned her attention back to her desk and the work spread out on the surface. Stacks of paperwork she couldn't concentrate on to save her life. Yet, she couldn't take any more time off work.

"Oh, you're back." A familiar voice made her turn to see one of the ladies from another department standing at her cubicle. The woman was nice enough, though she had a way of wanting a chat when Nevaeh was busiest, or in this case, most unwilling to talk. She also was known to eat the nastiest lunches she brought with her, leftovers from her dinners the night before, and she stunk up the lunchroom so often that Nevaeh now took lunch at her desk.

Nevaeh offered as much of a smile as she could muster under the circumstances. "Yes, this is my first day back."

"You don't look like you got much of a tan on your vacation."

"Oh. I'm a believer in sunscreen."

"Ah. Good to see you." The woman moved on, and Nevaeh was glad she hadn't probed her further. The topic of her trip was one she did not wish to discuss. What was there to say anyway? *I ended up being protected by a special ops unit who was looking for my brother, fell for a gorgeous captain on the team and then left with the promise that they were going to get Antonio back from the guys who kidnapped him ten years ago…*

She moved some papers around and calculated some sums for a project. Then she ended up staring at the wall again. Her cubicle was near the breakroom, and the odor of asparagus wafted out, letting her know her coworker was microwaving her meal.

Nevaeh's stomach twisted, and she reached for her ice water.

She was worthless here at work, but she couldn't go home either. Facing her parents with a mopey face would only alert them that something had happened, and she wasn't ready to talk about it.

When she drew the crackers serving as her own lunch out of her desk drawer, she pulled up a search engine on her phone. For a moment, she considered searching for information on Antonio. But what could possibly be new in his case? She'd hear about it first if there was anything.

Instead, she punched in *Nash Sullivan.*

A photo of him in the Texas Ranger gear of hat and boots hit her screen, and she gulped back a gasp of emotion. Seeing those dark eyes, so serious, and that solemn mouth of his, had her stomach doing flip-flops. Why did she have to have such a reaction to the man? Even in another decade, she wouldn't have forgotten the way Nash made her feel.

He'd peeled away so much of her armor, that protective layer had kept her heart shielded all this time. It was still there in a sense but thinking of Nash already had her feeling more vulnerable—as if she could finally reveal her true inner softness to someone.

To Nash.

She read over the few details there were associated with Nash, but it only said he was a lieutenant in the Texas Rangers division in Houston and then Waco.

She pressed her lips together and closed out of the page. Her crackers lay on her desk, untouched. She took up staring at her wall again. What had happened when they went after Antonio? Something must have gone wrong—was Nash okay? Or the others? Was Antonio?

It was too much to linger on. She stood and went through the office, responding to the friendly waves she got from some of her coworkers even as she wanted to snarl at them to leave her alone.

When she got outside, it was raining, something rare for this time of year. But the cooler air was welcome on her face, and she breathed in deeply, trying to gather her emotions.

The entire ordeal was confusing as hell. One minute she was excited about getting her brother back after all this time, and that was shot through with moments of total arousal thinking about Nash.

Standing under the overhang of the roof, she stayed out of the worst of the wet, but the droplets speckled her forearms, cooling her flesh, which she could use right now. Thinking about Nash had her entirely too worked up.

It was a short affair, born of her need for comfort and Nash's need to offer it. Nothing was real, not the emotions weaving through her heart and not the hope of ever seeing him again. Most likely, she'd find another pair of Texas Rangers on her doorstep telling her they still knew nothing of Antonio. It was something she'd learned to live with years ago, and could again, given the time. But she probably wouldn't ever set eyes on Nash Sullivan again. He'd be someone lingering only in her dreams, making her wake burning with the fire of his remembered touch.

Listening to the rain soothed her. What she had to do was appreciate the time she'd shared with Nash. As far as Antonio went, it was important to be grateful that anybody would even continue a search for her brother. The Ranger Ops team had put their lives on the line for him — for her and her parents. For that, she was thankful.

And in some ways, the experience had left her with the realization that she really needed to search for some happiness for herself. She ran her hands over her forearms, wiping off the raindrops.

The journey — and Nash — had taught her a lot in a short time.

If she didn't grab hold of life and make it better, who would?

* * * * *

"Back in Texas and shit just keeps getting better and better," Nash muttered as he and his men gathered around the table. Their poses might vary, but they all eyed him the same way.

Woody sat with his elbows on the table and his hands in his hair. "It's not our fault he didn't want to return, man. You know that, right?"

"Yeah, I know. It was what I feared could happen, and it fucking did." Nash still felt like punching shit.

"It happens all the time — people getting kidnapped and forced into a new life grow accustomed to it and won't leave." Lennon had suffered a nasty bump on the head but only had a mild concussion and had spent his time back on American soil at his local drinking hangout with his twin. Linc didn't look like he'd imbibed a single drop of alcohol, though — the man was as bright and alert as ever. If a gunman stepped into this room right now, Linc would be the first to draw his weapon.

Jess pushed out a sigh. "It's not what any family wants to hear. Have you talked to the Vincents yet, Sully?"

Nash ground his teeth. "No." He didn't have any reason to wait, other than he wanted to make a thousand percent certain that Antonio hadn't come searching for them to get him out of Mexico. But he hadn't. Cavanagh and Woody had seen him with their own eyes, back with Lopez, though after the fire, they were in a different location.

The mission was dead. A dead fucking body wrapped in plastic and duct tape and reeking of despair.

He shook his head. He hadn't told Nevaeh because he couldn't face her. How to tell the woman that he'd raised her hopes for nothing and now it was best to consider her brother dead, after all? He might as well be — he was dead to his birth family.

The table was silent as Sully thought over his role here. He looked up. "I'll go over there and talk to her this afternoon. But there's more, guys."

"Why am I getting a heavy feeling here, like our dad just took away Christmas?" Woody's joke didn't hold a bit of humor.

"It started with the comms unit. I reported to Downs that I need new equipment, and he told me that Homeland doesn't think we need the Ranger Ops unit at all — that Knight Ops is enough for the South."

They stared at him. Cavanagh pushed away from the table. "For fuck sakes!"

"Are you fucking serious, man? Where were the Knights when we were at the Sabine up to our asses in explosives? I didn't see them anywhere, did you, Jess?" Woody looked to his teammate.

"Dude, this is bullshit. So if Homeland is sayin' we aren't essential to OFFSUS, then what does that mean for Ranger Ops?" Lennon, even despite the blow to the head, was still sharp enough to ask the all-important question.

Nash gave a light shake of his head. "It means we continue to operate as usual until we're told our fun as ended."

"Shit. So much for fucking job security." Cavanagh stood, walked to the window and stood staring out of the slits in the blinds.

"Look, I know it doesn't make for great morale, but we have to make the most of it. We're still a unit, we're still fucking in charge of saving the world, okay?" Nash stood too. "I'll be in touch. Don't go far. I have a bad feeling about those ten units dispatched to Fort Worth."

He got several nods of agreement to his command, but he didn't stick around. He had his own mission, and that was paying a visit to Nevaeh. She deserved as much—he should have done it days ago. He'd just been reluctant to deliver the bad news until he had a final verdict on the matter.

Antonio was never coming home. He'd made his choice.

Nash checked the time and then slid behind the wheel of his Jeep. Describing the dread he felt wasn't even possible.

Just get it over with.

He knew where Nevaeh worked. Interrupting her during the day wasn't on his agenda, but he planned to wait in the parking lot and take her someplace quiet in order to break the news. He'd done such a thing many times in his past as a Texas Ranger and before that working as a state trooper. He'd told many people their loved ones had died in crashes or shootings—but not once had it been involving a person he knew.

Or had been intimate with.

He drove into the parking lot of her workplace and looked up at the windows, wondering if she had a nice office. With her quiet manner, he could see her sitting in front of a computer crunching numbers all day. He also knew that she chose to hide from the world, and accounting was the perfect vocation to do that. Yet what he knew about Nevaeh was so different.

She was strong, smart… and could be downright mouthy.

The thought brought a smile to his lips. He searched the parking lot for her vehicle and spotted the small red car with a sassy spoiler. He parked a couple spaces down from it and then cut the engine. Time passed. He wished he could say he wasn't sitting there with a hard-on, reliving all their moments together down in Mexico, but he fucking was.

Dammit, how was he going to keep his hands off her when he saw her again? Looking into her eyes would be the end of him. In the week since he'd seen her, he realized something big.

He wanted more with her. To pick her up and take her out to dinner. To park someplace secluded and look at the stars. All the things couples did while getting to know each other. They'd put the cart before the horse, so to speak, by sleeping together first, but that didn't make his feelings any less obvious to him.

He glanced up as people began to file out of the office building. He sat forward, staring at the faces, none of which were Nevaeh's. He was about to go searching for her, when she emerged, one of the last stragglers, carrying a purse and dressed in office attire of a slim skirt and a blouse. A closer look showed him that the buttons strained across her full breasts.

Hell, he was fully hard now.

He got out. When she spotted him, her eyes flew open wide. Her step faltered, and then she stopped, looking about to pass out.

"Fuck." He rushed forward and took her by the arm. "Lean on me. Here." He got her to his Jeep and helped her inside. When he jumped in the driver's side, she sat with her hands knotted. He searched her gaze, seeing so many hopes and dreams he was about to dash. But also, she projected a resignation he wasn't ready to address.

"Are you okay? Do you need anything? Water?" he asked.

She shook her head. Christ, she was stunning. Whether it was seeing her in her natural settings and knowing she was still drop-dead gorgeous or just his libido reacting to seeing her again, he didn't know.

When she sank her teeth into her lower lip, he latched his gaze to her mouth. The feel of those plump lips... He nearly groaned.

"What did you find out? Nash, you can't hold back anymore. I've been dying for a week, barely functioning. Just tell me he's dead so I can work through it and go on living my life."

His chest burned. Reaching across the console, he took her by the hand and squeezed it. "He's not dead. But Nevaeh... We had him, and he turned back."

There. It was out. He'd managed to say the words aloud.

For a moment, she just stared at him. God, he wanted to gather her to his chest and hold her. Before he could drag her across the seat into his lap, she spoke.

Her quiet words were barely audible. "He... turned back? He refused to come with you?"

Nash nodded. When she pulled her hand from his grasp, he realized he was frantically rubbing the back of her hand with his thumb in an effort to comfort her.

She raised a shaky hand to her face. "What does it mean now?"

He didn't want to say the words, but her expression told him that she already knew it. She was only seeking confirmation.

"It means he remains where he is, and you do your best to move on with your life."

She nodded, going pale. "What do I tell my parents?" Before he could think of how to answer, she said, "Maybe I'll just leave it as is, say nothing. They

157

still have hope that one day he will return to them, and I won't dash that for them."

"You know them best, darlin'."

Her head snapped up, and she looked into his eyes. "Nash..."

"I'm so sorry, Nevaeh. So fucking sorry. I tried my best — I had him. I had him to the vehicle, but he turned and ran back into the building. I... failed. And I'm sorry." His voice cracked, and it was her turn to offer comfort.

She grabbed his hand and threaded their fingers. Catching his eye, she said, "It isn't your fault. You did everything you could. Now at least he knows we were still searching for him, that he wasn't forgotten..." She broke off and straightened her spine in her tough-woman act. Well, she wasn't doing it alone.

"Shit. C'mere." Here he was, pulling her into his lap again. It seemed the perfect place for her, and his arms wrapping around her was the most natural thing in the world.

* * * * *

"Tell me what you're thinking." Nash's voice was a low rumble in his chest.

"I'm shocked, to be sure. But... I'm not totally surprised. You warned me this could happen." She looked up into his eyes. "I guess we just keep living our lives, as we have been. But I can move forward now, in a way I couldn't really before. Just knowing he's alive helps."

"What about your parents? Will you tell them?" He traced the length of her spine with his fingertips, sending warmth through her.

"I need to think more on that. Knowing he's alive but doesn't want to come home to them... that would probably break them even more. I'll have to think of all angles before I decide."

He nodded. "Good plan."

"I'm sorry you risked your life. You didn't fail, though, Nash. You and your men are amazing."

Giving a slow shake of his head, he said, "I can't believe you. You're comforting me when it should be me comforting you. Dammit, I knew you were special, but this..." He leaned in and gently brushed his lips across hers, once, twice. Then he pulled away. "Now that this is over, I want to talk to you about other things."

Those other things couldn't be how her body was reacting to sitting in his lap, could it? That dark heat she knew so well when it came to Nash was slithering low through her body again, curling between her thighs like the most forbidden and exciting touch.

She felt breathless when she answered, "What things?"

"Well, for one, I want to see you. Get to know you. I know where you work and what you drive, but I don't know how you drive or how you look when you crunch numbers. I don't know if you enjoy your job."

Touched that he would want to learn these things, she smiled. "I do like my job. Sometimes the people try me, but that's every office environment, right?"

"It's any job, yeah. But I have to say these guys I'm working with…" He looked into her eyes, and she felt closer to him yet. "We had a sort of breakthrough. A bonding moment back there in Mexico."

"Tell me about it."

"My communication device stopped working when we got in there, and I was giving orders only by using hand signals, which meant we couldn't exactly operate the way we'd planned by spreading out. But by the time things really got intense, the guys were all using the hand signals. It became a language we were all in tune with."

"I don't know how you do it, Nash. Your work is something I could never do."

"That's not true—you went to Mexico on your own reconnaissance mission." His lips tilted upward at one corner.

"I had to find out what I could. Good thing I ran into a man who would fill me in." She reached up and smoothed her fingers over his angular jaw, watching his eyes as they darkened by the minute.

He began to lean toward her again, but she stopped him.

"This chemistry between us — it's real isn't it?" she asked.

"Oh yeah." He slid his hand beneath her hair and tangled his fingers against her skull, cradling her while he searched her eyes. "I have some horses boarded nearby. I don't have a place big enough to keep them yet, but I'm working on it. I'd like to take you to see them. Do you ride?"

"I used to when I was a young girl, with Antonio."

"Good memories, I'm sure. Will you come with me right now?"

She laughed. "Now?"

"Yeah. I'm free, but who knows for how long. I want to spend time with you before I'm called to some other duty."

"I'll come with you, but I need to change out of this skirt and heels if I'm going to walk or ride."

Running his thumb back and forth over her lower lip, he moved in by slow degrees. When he finally kissed her, she was more than ready — burning for him. She wrapped her arms around his neck and clung as he plundered her mouth like he owned every inch of her.

Thing was, she wasn't so sure he didn't.

Suddenly, he broke the kiss and lifted her. She giggled as he plopped her back into the passenger's seat. "Your car should be safe enough here."

"Yes," she said. "It's a good part of town." As he started the Jeep and rolled out of the parking lot, he turned in the direction of her house. "You know where I live?"

He shot her a glance. "I kinda know everything, darlin'." His smoldering expression hinted at knowing more—like exactly what turned her on, starting with that look on his handsome face.

During the drive, she noticed more things about him, such how the veins down his forearms snaked in such an enticing way. Those long fingers wrapped around the steering wheel made her insides tense up too. And he wasn't just driving—he was hyper-alert. No wonder he had spotted Antonio during that other mission. The man missed nothing, it seemed.

When they reached her small neighborhood and he pulled up outside of the home she shared with her parents, he cut the engine and looked to her. "Could I come in? I'd like to meet your parents."

That threw her for a loop-de-loop. "Um, of course. I'd like that. Just..." She pressed her lips together.

"I won't say a word about your brother. It isn't my place, darlin', and I'm not out to cause more hurt."

She nodded and got out. How was it that having a gorgeous man beside her made the world appear so different? Changed, almost. The sad little neighborhood suddenly showed off the birds

162

chirping in trees and shrubbery and little kids biking at the end of the street.

She'd always tried to see the beauty in the world without Antonio, but now... knowing he was at least alive and sharing a planet with her left her feeling lightened. Maybe telling her parents would help them see this way as well.

When she opened the screen door, Nash held it back for her. She led him into the house, and her mother came from the kitchen. The scents of dinner wafted out.

Her mother came to a stop. Her eyes widened, and Nevaeh was thankful Nash wasn't in uniform of any kind. If her momma saw another Texas Ranger in her house, she'd probably run out the back door screaming.

Nash made the first move. "Hello, I'm Nash Sullivan."

"We're friends," Nevaeh jumped in.

"Hello. Nice to meet you." Her mother sliced a look Nevaeh's way, and she hoped Nash couldn't read her mother's expression the way she was. Her mother obviously thought Nash was just as hunky as Nevaeh did, judging by the light smile that touched her lips.

"Nash has horses, and he's taking me riding."

"Oh, how nice. You haven't done that in a while. Is it still raining?"

"It stopped on our way here," Neveah said.

Her momma glanced over her work attire. "You'd better get changed. Would you two like to eat with us before you go? There's plenty of spaghetti."

Nash smiled. "I think we'll grab something on the way but thank you for the invite. Next time."

Nevaeh's stomach pitched and leaped like she was on a carnival ride. *There's going to be a next time.*

Reluctant to leave these two together to make small-talk while she changed, she finally slipped off to her room to put on jeans, a T-shirt and boots. The nights were still a little on the cool side, and she didn't know how long they'd be out, so she grabbed a light jacket as well.

When she emerged from her room, she saw her mother laughing at something Nash had said. Nevaeh centered on her mother's happy face, something she didn't see every day.

Maybe her mother needed to see her moving forward with her life, having the things a young woman did, like a boyfriend and fun dates to ride horses. It struck Nevaeh that in many ways, she had contributed to the sad cloud hanging over their family.

"I'm ready," she announced.

Nash turned to her and when his gaze landed on her, his dark eyes hooded with the look she remembered all too well from their stolen moments in Mexico.

He wanted her.

God, she wanted him too.

When she hugged her mom goodbye, the woman put her lips to Nevaeh's ear. "He's hot."

Lordy, she hoped Nash hadn't overheard that exchange. She nodded and pulled away from her mother. They made it to the Jeep and Nash had started the engine before he turned to her with a wide smile.

"So... you think I'm hot?"

Chapter Eight

Nash pulled into the small ranch that belonged to his friend Lang. It was good to see it unchanged. Though it had only been a few weeks since he'd been here to see his horses and ride, Nash felt as if it had been a lot longer.

Between the Ranger Ops' formation and their trip to Mexico to go after Nevaeh's brother, he'd changed a lot. He wondered how long it would take for his buddy to see the changes and comment on them.

Not long, since he was bringing a pretty woman by to meet him.

Not just pretty—stunning. When Nevaeh had come out of her bedroom in casual attire, Nash's cock had stirred. It was impossible not to envision stripping off every garment and leaving kisses all over her as he went.

She slid her hands into the back pockets of her jeans and looked around. "It's great here. You said it's your friend's?"

"Yeah, he's a Texas Ranger too, old school to the core, but we have a lot in common."

"Does he know you're bringing me?"

"No. But he won't mind, trust me. C'mon." He started toward the house with her at his side. But that didn't feel right, so he took her hand, meshing their fingers.

He felt her give a little tremble and looked over at her. "There's nothing to be nervous about."

"I'm not nervous."

His mind went straight to the idea that she might have had a reaction to simply holding his hand, and his heart gave a happy leap.

The ranch-style house looked as neat and orderly as always, the landscaping trimmed and a comfy chair on the porch where Lang liked to sit out and sip a beer or two every night. The single chair might look lonely to some, but Nash knew his friend better than that. The man had earned what peace he found after decades in the Texas Rangers and after grieving two wives.

Nash had always planned to have something similar, without the heartbreak, of course. But stepping up to the door with Nevaeh at his side gave him new ideas.

What if there were two chairs? And maybe a kid's bicycle or two in the yard?

He rang the doorbell and glanced down at Nevaeh. Just then the door opened, and Lang stood there in worn jeans and boots, his hat pulled low. He pushed it back as he took in the sight on his doorstep.

167

"Not surprised you turned up. Good timing too. Those horses are missin' ya." He turned his gaze to Nevaeh. "And I see you brought a pretty girl by too."

She made a sound in her throat and flushed at his compliment.

"This is Nevaeh. Nevaeh, meet Lang, one of the greatest Texas Rangers since Frank Hamer. Thought we'd have a visit and then go ridin'."

Lang chuckled. "Nash exaggerates, but I'm sure you've figured that out by now. Come in and sit a spell. I was just fixin' to have some tea." To Nevaeh, he said, "I hope you're not opposed to a dash of whiskey in the mix?"

Smiling, she shook her head.

Lang led them to the kitchen, where he had a pitcher of tea on the counter as well as a bottle of his favorite whiskey. He dumped a small amount into each glass and then filled each with tea.

Nash accepted his glass and brought it to his lips. "Lang's got a way of welcoming a person." He sipped, savoring the honey touched with a slight burn of alcohol.

"I reckon we wiped out a lot of tea and whiskey together, that's true." Lang slid his gaze from Nevaeh to Nash. A true happiness shone in his friend's eyes, echoing what Nash was feeling right now.

"Let's go out onto the deck. We can see the horses from there," Lang suggested.

168

With drinks in hand, they followed him outside. The deck ran the length of the house and wrapped around a side.

Nevaeh let out a small sigh at the view of the paddocks with the horses grazing, their manes and tails waving in the breeze that came off the fields beyond. Nash had always longed for a place just like this, but now that feeling was even stronger.

"It's beautiful here," she said.

"A beauty who appreciates beauty. What are you doing with this chump?" Lang's question made her laugh, and they both watched as she tossed her head back, giving them a healthy view of all that thick hair that had Nash entranced from the beginning.

Lang gave him a knowing smile, and Nash nodded, turning his attention to his drink.

Nevaeh went to lean against the railing and look out at the horses. "I'm eager to ride. It's been too long, and I didn't realize how much I missed it until now."

"A real Texas girl. Nice to see. What did you say your last name was?" Lang asked.

"Vincent."

His friend's gaze shot to Nash's, and they exchanged a moment of mental communication. Lang was sharp and put two and two together pretty damn quick. Nash figured at some point, he'd be sitting right here on this deck relating the tale of how he and Nevaeh had come to this point after bonding in Mexico.

169

Bonding... Until now, Nash hadn't thought about it in those terms, yet there was no question in his mind or heart.

She and Lang chatted as they finished their drinks. Then they all walked down to the stables together. As she proved she hadn't forgotten how to saddle a horse, Lang waved Nash over.

"Hold on tight to her. She's just what you need."

"How do you know?" Why was Nash's throat suddenly tight?

"I was lucky enough to find that twice in my life. I know." He clapped Nash's shoulder. "Have a good ride. Don't forget to close the gate when you're done."

"I won't." He watched Lang make his way back to the house. Nevaeh mounted and tested the horse with a few tugs on the reins.

"This one's eager to go. C'mon, slow poke," she called to Nash.

Damn, this woman had taught him things.

All his life he'd considered himself a hard-ass. It was what made him a good state trooper, then a Texas Ranger and finally landed him in this position with OFFSUS. He tried to let the people close to him know they were important, but Nevaeh had said goodbye to her brother and never seen him again. Nash didn't want that weight on him from holding back with Lang, so he hurried after him and pulled his friend in for an embrace before returning to his horse and mounting.

She tossed a smile Nash's way, and happiness spread over him. If this was how his life could be, then he was ready to get started. What more could he need? He had work he loved and a woman who rocked his world.

Hold on tight to her.

Lang's words reverberated in his mind as he and Nevaeh rode out across the field to the trail that cut around the perimeter of the ranch.

* * * * *

Nevaeh drew the horse to a stop and looked around. "This doesn't seem like the Texas I know." Her voice held a tinge of awe, but she didn't care — the ranch was beautiful. She felt transported to another country, maybe France. The lush fields speckled with wildflowers and the creek cutting through the property in a lazy arc invited visions of picnics on the banks or spreading out a blanket and...

She stole a glance at Nash. He looked as comfortable in a saddle as he did in camo and cargos.

"This place comes pretty damn close to perfect." His gaze landed on her. "As far as land goes."

She felt the caress of those words, the subtle compliment that had her cheeks warming.

Nash pointed. "Let's head down there. It's a nice spot to let the horses drink."

She nodded and they meandered along the shore of the creek, which was wide enough to make a child happy with room to splash or catch a frog or two.

When Nash stopped and dismounted, she looked on, admiring the cut of his muscles and the pull of his jeans against his thighs. He turned to her with a smile and held out a hand. She took it and slipped from the saddle, straight into his arms.

He held her fast to his hard body for several breathless heartbeats. But he didn't kiss her, like she hoped for. He just stared down at her, an expression in his eyes that she couldn't read.

When he released her, he checked the horses, setting them loose.

"Do we need to hobble or tie them?" she asked.

"They know this place well. They won't go anywhere."

Unable to hold back the need rising inside her, she stepped up to Nash and slid her arms around his neck. Her breasts pressed to his steely chest, making her nipples tighten.

He planted his hands on her waist. His brow creased and she reached up to smooth it with her fingertips. "What has you worrying?" she asked so softly that the babble of the creek almost covered her words.

"Just wonderin' what I did to deserve you lookin' at me that way."

This man was about as humble as they came. Her heart was tripping fast. "You know I have a hard time keeping my hands off you."

The corner of his lips twitched but didn't come close to a smile. "I wish I had more to give you."

She tangled her fingers into the hair at the base of his neck. "I'm not asking for much."

"You deserve everything. I can't even promise that I won't be called out this afternoon and have to cut our time short."

"Then you better not waste anymore time talking." She went on tiptoe, pulling his head down to seal her lips over his. At first, she felt the tension in him at their discussion, but when she pressed closer, that flowed away.

With a noise breaking from his throat, he yanked her against him, bending to the task of kissing her.

Damn, the man could kiss. Every inch of her was on fire in seconds, and she rubbed herself shamelessly against him.

A growl escaped him, and he scooped her up and lowered her to the ground, sinking his tongue between her lips again and again on the way down. She clutched at him, parting her thighs to draw him against her neediest spot.

"I've missed you so much," she rasped between hot sweeps of his tongue.

He eased his hand under her T-shirt, wasting no time in cupping her breast and finding her hard

173

nipple. She squeaked in pleasure and arched up for more.

"I can't hold back from taking you." His eyes glimmered as he moved his hand to the waist of her jeans. She reached for his belt buckle, and with a series of tugs and pulls, they managed to get their clothes off. The grasses were soft against her skin, not that she cared. She just wanted Nash buried inside her.

Spreading her thighs, she gave him a look she was certain matched the hunger in his own eyes. He stroked his cock from base to tip, and a bead of precum gathered there.

She swiped her thumb over it and brought it to her lips.

"Fucking hell, you're sexy." His eyes lidded as he watched her lick his juices from her thumb.

A groan left him. He plastered himself to her, the head of his swollen cock at her slick folds as he crushed his lips to hers. The kiss was five-alarm, blazing out of control. She wouldn't be surprised to see flames around them. Using her ankles on his backside, she yanked him in — inside her.

He filled her in a slippery rush, stretching her in all the right ways. Crying out, she locked onto the sensation even as her heart thundered *yes, yes, yes.*

Hell yes.

She bucked upward, and he sank an inch deeper. They shared a moan.

"Christ, you feel good, darlin'. Grip me. That's it," he crooned as her inner walls clutched at his length.

He slid out and shoved home again. Her whimpers mixed with his guttural growls, and soon she was shaking in his arms, her orgasm just on the horizon. "I'm so close. Oh my God." She shuddered as she began to peak. "Come with me, Nash. I want to feel your cum dripping out of me."

Her words seemed to spike his release. He ground his hips fast and hard, burrowing deeper with every stroke. Her world shattered, and stars exploded behind her eyes as ecstasy struck. When the first hot splash of his cum hit her pussy, she curled closer to him, wanting more than just pleasure.

Because she was in love with him.

Rocking his hips to the rhythm of his groans, he fixed his stare on her. The fireworks in the depths of his eyes turned her on as much as feeling him explode inside her.

"Nash." His name came out as a breathless whisper. "Kiss me."

He slanted his mouth across hers, dragging a few more pulsations from her pussy with the feel of his tongue. She dug her nails into his shoulders and kissed him back with all the emotion building inside her.

As his hips gave a final pump, he cradled her against his chest.

Her senses returned after another minute or so, and she felt at one with the universe in a way that made her want to dance naked around a field or something equally as crazy.

She was in love.

"Nash."

He pulled back and half-rolled off her, looking into her eyes. Damn, he was a gorgeous man. She traced his square jaw with a fingertip, marveling at how such a hard man, a man who was capable of protecting their country, could be so tender with her.

She had to say what was on her mind. "You're worried that you won't have the time to give, yet you've taken advantage of every minute we've had together."

He nodded. "God help me, I couldn't stop myself in Mexico. Something about you..." His gaze wandered over her hair, which he twisted around his fingers, and finally rested on her eyes.

"Something about you too," she whispered, her throat closing off.

Leaning in, he brushed his lips over her forehead. "I'm trying to take it slow with you, but damn if I don't want to wake up next to you in my bed."

Her stomach gave a wild dip of joy. "Well... maybe I wanna wake up in your bed."

When Nash Sullivan gave one of his rare grins, she couldn't hold back—she fell the rest of the way in love with him.

* * * * *

"As much as I want to fuck you until you can't sit comfortably in that saddle, I'll let you get dressed." Nash handed Nevaeh's top to her. She took it with a coy smile and pulled it over her head. Even clothed, the effect she had on him was devastating. He might as well have been caught in a bomb blast.

He gave a light shake of his head. Taking it slow with Nevaeh seemed essential. He was a tactical guy, a planner.

But even he knew that sometimes you made shit up on the fly, and that seemed to be the case with this enticing woman.

Still, he couldn't fill his Jeep with all her belongings and sweep her off to his apartment either. He had to give her the time to understand his life — and back out if she couldn't handle it.

Start slow, he thought. *Dinner, a movie, maybe cop a feel or three…*

Then kiss her goodbye at her front door and text her when he got home.

All this seemed the right course for a couple that was newly dating. But even he was aware of his feelings for her enough to know their bond had run deep from the start. Their first date had been over tamales in a hostel room and solidified when he broke through her tough exterior time and again.

He scuffed at his jaw, feeling the rasp of five o'clock shadow. Hell, what now? According to

177

Downs, he might not even have a job next week, if the Pentagon decided Ranger Ops wasn't needed. He'd be lucky to get his position back as Texas Ranger—those spots were snatched up quickly. He knew for a fact Woody's position had already been filled in Austin.

Nash had no business asking more from Nevaeh right now. Slow was best.

Essential.

Dammit.

Just looking at the beautiful woman half turned from him, her hair tumbling over her shoulder as she bent to hitch on her cowgirl boot, had him aching with something sweeter than he'd ever felt in his life.

As she straightened, she shot him a grin. Thank God she didn't know all the thoughts pouring through his head or she'd run for her life.

He whistled to the horses, and they came trotting back to them. Nevaeh combed her fingers through her mount's mane, cooing to it in a soft tone. When she caught Nash staring at her, she gave him a quizzical smile.

"Do you think I'm crazy baby-talking a horse?"

He shook his head. "Not at all. I think you're beautiful and sweet to the core. I have no damn clue what you're doing with me, but I'm not going to argue."

Her smile and the glow in her eyes—hell, the glow all over her body after that orgasm that had shaken them both—had him falling hard, fast and deep.

They rode back to the paddock in quiet companionship. Along the way, he pointed out the hidden head of a trail he'd take her on next time, and that made her smile. Damn, he wanted to put that happiness in her eyes every damn second of her life.

As soon as he slid out of the saddle to open the gate and lead the horses through, he sensed a charge in the air. The second his sixth sense kicked in, his phone vibrated with a text.

He pulled it out and stared at the screen. Lang's message flashed into view.

Called in to Fort Worth. Be sure to close the gate.

"Asshole," he said softly and with affection at his friend's repeated order, as if Nash would ever forget to care for the horses.

It felt odd, too, knowing that he wasn't expected on the scene. He stared at the screen another second before looking up to find Nevaeh looking at him with a crease between her brows.

"What is it?" she asked.

"Lang was called out to an incident. We'll just get the horses settled and then lock up for him."

She nodded. While they removed the saddles and tack from the horses and set them free in the paddock, Nash didn't realize how silent he was, or that it was causing concern in Nevaeh.

She rested a hand on his arm. "Are you okay?"

179

"My alarms are buzzin'," he said at once. Confiding that was new for him.

"What can you do? I can call a cab and get myself home if you want to go to the scene."

He shook his head. "No, I'll drive you home. I'm not a Texas Ranger anymore, and they're covered. They don't need me. It's just odd, knowing about a call and not being there for it."

They left after he checked the gate one last time. In the Jeep, he considered putting on the scanner to hear what was going on, but he refrained. Nevaeh didn't need to hear that and be on edge with worry.

When they reached her home, he parked out front and turned to her. "I'm glad you came riding with me today."

She smiled. "Me too. When will I see you again?"

"Soon. I just have this feeling, and I think I'm going to head to the scene whether I'm wanted or not."

"All right. Will you let me know you're okay?"

"As soon as possible." He leaned in and kissed her, and her lips softened under his in invitation that he ached to explore. But he had to get this weight off his shoulders first and check in.

She drew away, her eyes shining, and opened the door. "I'll talk to you soon."

He nodded. Driving away from her was a wrench for him, but his mind turned immediately to his task at hand. He put in a call to the station and got the details. An address in a lowly part of the city, which wasn't a surprise. They often dealt with robberies, shootings and more in that section.

After some considerable drive time, Nash's molars ached from grinding his teeth. His phone rang, and he pressed a button to put it on speakerphone. The streets were clogged with traffic, and frustration was mounting. He barked out, "Sullivan."

"It's Shaw." Woody's drawl came thickly through the speakers. "Did you hear?"

"Hear what? Did we get a call?" Why wasn't he getting it first? If Ranger Ops was needed, he should have been notified long ago.

"No. I was talking about the robbery and the shooting."

Nash's stomach hollowed out. He fucking knew he should have been there. Another gun on the area, especially his, would have probably stopped someone from being wounded or a fatality.

"I haven't heard. I'm on my way there now."

"You're close with Lang, right?"

Dread crept over Nash, tightening the skin on his skull. "Yeah," he heard himself say from far away and through a sudden drumming in his ears.

Woody was silent a moment.

"What do you know, Woody? Fucking say it." He didn't want to hear it, because he already knew.

"Lang was shot and killed about ten minutes ago."

Fury rushed Nash's system, and he slammed his fist into the dash. "Goddammit!"

His friend, mentor, an older brother or father figure. Shot and killed, when he should have been tucked safely behind his desk, resting his arthritic knees.

What a fucking waste of a life.

"I'm sorry, Sully. I wanted to be the first to tell you, so you weren't blindsided." Woody's voice rang with regret.

"Thanks," he grated out. "I'm almost there now. I'll be in touch." Nash's throat clogged with the need to bellow his rage. He clamped his fingers on the wheel. The minute he got that shooter in his sights, the man was fucking dust, because Nash was going to pump him full of so much lead.

Dammit. Lang. Why Lang?

He didn't go to calls often anymore. Was it Nash's teasing about being a desk jockey that had sent him there?

"Fucking hell!" he yelled into the quiet of his vehicle. All these years he'd looked up to Lang. Had he told him so? Had he given the man the farewell he should have? Hell, he'd thought they were just riding out on the trails and he'd see his buddy in an hour or two. Life was abrupt and cruel at times, and this was one of those.

Nash yanked his hat lower to cover his emotion, even though nobody was here to witness it. His first real bond with another Texas Ranger had been with Lang. Now that was broken, shattered forever in a senseless crime.

Even as the loss hit him like a blast, he realized another man had been there for him. Woody had called to break the news to him, and that said a hell of a lot about what Nash had in Ranger Ops.

When he reached the scene of the robbery, his phone began to blow up with calls and texts from Jess, Cavanagh, Lennon and Linc.

Nash didn't read the texts or listen to the voicemails—he knew what they said already.

What those men really said was that they were there for Nash, in the same way Lang had been all these years. He'd traded one team for another, and in that moment, he knew no matter what dangerous missions they faced, they'd be doing it together.

Chapter Nine

The problem with Texas was the weather never did cooperate. Either it was storming its balls off and cold when it should be summer weather, or it was a perfect eighty degrees with a cloudless blue sky when you were burying your good friend. Nash sent a glare toward the sky. Goddammit, it should be raining to reflect his mood.

The bugler stood straight and tall, the notes of *Taps* rolling over Nash and forcing him to blink back his emotion. Lang's coffin was lowered into the ground and the flag folded, along with a sash someone's wife had embroidered with the Texas Rangers symbol. Each of the men Lang had worked with signed it.

Nash clenched his fist at his side, still feeling that marker in his hand as he'd scribbled his name on a note to his friend for the last time. Today, they were sending him off in style.

One of the men stepped up to the hole in the ground, scooped up a handful of dirt and scattered it over the coffin.

Nash hung back, letting everyone go before him, buying more time. Lang wouldn't want him grieving for long—he'd tell him to grab life by the reins and ride on, and Nash intended to after today.

Seeing everyone had taken their turn saying farewell, he peered at the hole. Finality swept him.

Stepping forward, he sank his hand into the dirt. The dry, crumbly ground filled his fingers, a few grains escaping from between his knuckles. He stared down at the dirt-strewn coffin. Pain was a jagged edge in his chest.

"Behave yourself, man, ya hear? And don't worry about your horses—I'll make sure they have the care they need." Lang employed a guy to come and help anyway, and Nash would pay him to continue doing that duty. It was the least he could do.

As he opened his hand, releasing the dirt down into the hole, his throat closed off. Then he nodded hard, as if he was answering something Lang had told him. Since he knew just what his friend would be telling him—to give 'em hell, to live for pleasure and love hard—he would try his best to meet those expectations.

Swallowing the lump in his throat, he moved away from the hole, brushing off his hand on his suit pants. He headed toward the parking lot, and his phone vibrated.

It could be Nevaeh again, checking up on him. Her concern was touching, and damn if it didn't make him feel closer to her. To him, it seemed like one of those 'through good times and bad' moments they talked about at weddings.

He'd declined her offer to join him for the funeral, though, wanting to get through it alone. When he drew out his phone and glanced at the text from Woody, he was surprised to see an address there—nothing else.

He got behind the wheel of his Jeep. When he punched the number into his GPS, he started laughing.

Well, he wasn't exactly dressed for bowling, but he'd make do. Burning off some of the day's stress with Shaw was just what he needed. Maybe have a beer or two as well.

As he drove to the bowling alley, he stopped being mad at the weather for betraying him. Lang had been an important part of his life for years, and that wouldn't change. Nash wouldn't be the man he was today without that Texas Ranger's input. He'd shaped Nash from day one, primed him to be the best.

And he wouldn't let him down with Ranger Ops.

When he arrived at his destination and entered the bowling alley, he spotted not only Woody but the other guys as well. A grin spread over his face. They came forward to thump him on the back and grip hands with him in a bro-shake. Their support touched him.

Lennon gave Nash the once-over. "You forgot your bowling shirt."

He started to take off his jacket. "I'll remember next time." He rolled up the sleeves of his white dress

186

shirt and removed his tie. With his shirt collar unbuttoned and his best cowboy boots replaced with garish bowling shoes, he was comfortable enough to bowl a strike or two.

The guys had two lanes already and their names were up on the scoreboards. Nash stopped a moment, staring up at their combined names.

The six of them were a family, newly formed but no less important to each other.

And Nash was damn proud to be leading them all.

* * * * *

When Nevaeh stepped out of the office to see the hottest guy holding a beautiful bouquet of flowers, her heart tumbled. As she moved toward Nash, she got that weak-kneed feeling she always did around him.

He held out the flowers, and she took them, dropping her nose to inhale the sweet scents.

"Thank you." She lifted her gaze to his, and warmth bloomed in her core.

"I hope you don't have plans. I'd like to take you out."

She shook her head. "Not unless you call watching cooking shows with my parents plans."

He chuckled. "I think you can catch the reruns."

Excitement made her tingle. "Where are we going? Am I dressed okay?" Her office attire of black pants and a brightly-colored blouse wasn't exactly fit for extravagant dinners out or riding.

"You're perfect." He leaned in and kissed her lips, stealing her breath. When she inhaled again, she caught the notes of musk and man, the combination devastating to her.

Drawing back, he gave her one of those rare crooked smiles. He opened his mouth to say something but went still. "Damn," he said softly. He drew his phone out of his pocket and stared at the screen.

By his expression, she knew it wasn't what he wanted to see.

"What is it?" she asked.

"I'm called out, darlin'." His eyes met hers. "I'm sorry. I'm going to have to postpone tonight."

"I understand."

He cupped her cheek, and she felt the tension already humming through him, like he was a jet engine ready for takeoff. She placed her hand on his chest, over his strong heart. "Go," she said softly. "I'll be here when you get back."

"Damn, I don't know how I found you. You're damn perfect, you know that?" He stamped his mouth over hers, hard. Bruising.

Claiming.

She parted her lips on a gasp, and he plunged his tongue in, sweeping over hers with a promise that left her jittery and aching. When he pulled back as abruptly as he'd kissed her, he crushed her to his chest and bowed his nose to her hair. "I hate that this is how it will be, me leaving on a moment's notice."

"Nash, it's okay. I understand. My boyfriend's out saving the world. We'll have that date when you return." Going on tiptoe, she kissed him again with all the sweet longing inside her. "Be safe."

He released her, his hand still hovering around her waist as if he wanted to grab her back. He took a step off the sidewalk toward his vehicle. "I'll call you the minute I'm back."

"Okay." She clutched her flowers, since she couldn't hold the man who'd given them to her.

He reached his Jeep, and she watched him climb inside. Suddenly, he rolled down the passenger's window and leaned over to call out to her.

"Did you just call me your boyfriend?"

Her grin spreading across her face felt so good. "Yes, I did. Now go save the world, Nash."

Grinning back, he rolled the window up. She watched him drive away.

Yes, it was undeniable. She was in love with that man. Sure, they had hurdles to leap and plenty more get-to-know-you dates to experience, but that was like the cream filling in the donut for her.

Back in the house, she placed her flowers in water. When her mother came into the kitchen, she was surprised to find Nevaeh standing there. "Lovely flowers, but where's the man?"

"He got called out to work." She felt her brow crease with worry. What dangers would he be facing? She couldn't imagine barreling full-force into situations like that day after day. Surely, it would take a toll on the men and women who performed those duties. Nash seemed stoic, with a stiff upper lip. Though she didn't know everything there was to know about the man, she knew things affected him and he refused to talk about it.

Like losing his friend Lang or coming home without Antonio.

If she was going to be a good girlfriend, she needed to find ways to help him work through those rough points in his life and find peace.

Speaking of peace…

She turned to her mother. "Can I talk to you and Dad about something?"

At her serious tone, her mother eyed her. "Let's go sit down in the living room. Your father won't be dozing at this time of day."

Butterflies of nervousness hatched in Nevaeh's stomach. She took a calming breath and followed her mother. They sat on the sofa side by side with her father in the recliner. The moment stretched.

Nevaeh could still back out of telling them she'd gone to Mexico. She didn't have to stir things up yet again, as so many had done over the years. She looked down at her hands in her lap, confusion flooding her.

"What's going on, honey? You can always talk to us," her mother prompted, reaching over to touch Nevaeh's arm.

She looked between her parents. "That vacation I took... it was to Mexico."

Her mother sucked in a breath, and her father removed his glasses to pinch the bridge of his nose.

Nevaeh rushed on, "I just had to wrap things up in my mind. After those last Texas Rangers came to the house to question us, I just had to find some semblance of closure."

"And did you?" Her mother's voice was small.

Nevaeh nodded. "I think I did. I can move on with my life in a healthier way than I have been, and I feel like you two should as well. I want to see more smiles and hear more laughter around here. Mom, you love gardens and you've always wanted to visit Hawaii to see all their native plants. Maybe it's time for you and Dad to do that." All this time, Nevaeh had felt her parents had been talking about this trip but putting it off, almost afraid Antonio would come home if they left the house.

They couldn't live like this anymore.

Her mother searched her eyes. "I thought the change in you was due to that handsome young man of yours."

Nevaeh laughed. "Maybe it is a little. I'm happy with him. But it's more of a peace I feel inside, and I want both of you to feel too."

Her father placed his glasses back on his face and stared at her and her mother. "Well, Kathy, I guess you'd better get online and books us a vacation."

Her mother leaped off the couch and skipped over to the recliner, wrapping her arms around him. As her dad hugged her, he looked over her shoulder at Nevaeh. They shared a smile.

Nevaeh stood, wanting to give them some time alone to discuss their exciting new plans. Feeling lighter than she had in a long time, she drifted back into the kitchen, smiling at the sight of her flowers in the white vase. Hopefully soon she would be seeing the man who'd gifted them to her. She wrapped her arms around her middle and recalled the feel of his lips on hers.

* * * * *

"Damn, your shooting sucks as much as your bowling." Nash threw out to Jess, whose bullet had hit just left of center. The sparks of steel on steel flashed in the darkness as the lock that was his target dangled, half broken.

"I'd get a better shot if you weren't in my damn way," Jess volleyed back. He squeezed off the shot, this time shooting the lock off the door. All six of them were immediately on their feet and storming the entrance to the building.

As soon as Nash's boots touched the floorboards, he knew this was the place — his instincts were on.

"Jesus, look at this." Woody braced his legs wide, his rifle in hand at the ready as he scanned the space, taking in what they all were, which was illegal weapons spread over the table, along with enough cash to make men with security on their minds take a second glance.

"If only it wasn't a crime to keep all this money," Cavanagh drawled.

Woody grunted. "We kept a bunch of Hitler's personal items when we invaded the Eagle's Nest."

Nash huffed out a laugh. "Keep alert, guys. We might have missed some of those alarm wires."

"Not possible," Jess said. "I cut the whole system."

"Still best to be on alert. Split up." Raising a hand, Nash signaled for them to go in pairs. He and Shaw slinked through the warehouse, keeping on the defensive each time they rounded another huge crate. What Downs had sent them to find, though, was the mass amounts of illegal arms coming in packed inside crates of clothing.

On the backside of discovering the home base for these assholes was ambushing them when they returned from their latest shipment run. The guard at the gate had been an easy mark, and Lennon had taken him out cleanly after the man took aim at him.

"Don't fuck with the Ranger Ops," Nash said quietly. A chuckle sounded in his comms unit. It was brand new, and with luck it wouldn't crap out on him again.

Suddenly, a faint noise hit his ears. He jerked his head to the side. Woody went still, poised to shoot. Nash twitched his fingers, asking if he'd heard something.

Woody shook his head.

Nash stared at a crate. Lifting a hand, he felt along it. Sure enough, one of the wood panels was loose.

A fucking door.

To his men, he breathed out, "They're in the fucking crates."

Linc and Lennon rounded the huge crate, along with Jess and Cavanagh. Six weapons trained on the wood as Nash lifted a boot and kicked through the wood.

Chapter Ten

Nash's shoulders ached. His spine ached. Hell, even his hair ached. He wanted nothing more than a hot shower and a bed. Preferably one with Nevaeh in it, so after he gathered his strength, he could turn to her and —

On second thought, he had enough energy for *that*.

He stepped into the office to debrief, and Colonel Downs was waiting for him, leaning against his desk with his arms folded over his chest. "Captain Sullivan. You look like shit."

A grin ghosted across his face, but even that hurt. "At least I'm alive, sir."

"Pull up a chair."

Nash was accustomed to being drilled for information on whatever crime he'd just investigated, stopped or dealt with, but sitting down for it was entirely new.

He resisted a groan as his backside hit the seat. Either he was out of shape or the hand-to-hand combat he'd started — and finished — had gone on for longer than he remembered. Fighting for his life, he'd used every muscle group, and the way he felt, he'd dragged in a couple he didn't even have to use against his opponent too.

"I hope the other guy looks worse, Sullivan." Downs contemplated him, and something about the way he eyed him reminded Nash of Lang.

"The other guy's dead, sir. I hope I look a sight better."

A wry smile tipped Downs' lips. "I'd say you came out on top then. Keep talkin'."

At first, Nash's recounting of what had taken place back in that warehouse came in stilted bursts of words. But as he spoke, he began to relax until finally he was leaning against the back of his chair and the tale flowed freely. As he drew to a close, he realized just how cathartic the telling was.

And that it was a hell of a lot like shooting the shit with his old buddy Lang.

He pressed his fist to his mouth, taking a moment of silence for his fallen friend and thinking too on the way Lang had preached his patience and keeping hold of his temper. What Nash had learned these past months was how to use his anger to his benefit.

Colonel Downs cleared his throat, bringing Nash back to attention. He asked a few more details about what had resulted in one of the biggest illegal weapons seizes of the year.

"You know this has put Ranger Ops on the radar."

"Does it mean more job security for us?"

Downs ran his forefinger over his temple. "I hope to hell it does, but nothing's been said to me yet."

"Be a damn shame to cut us from OFFSUS. Didn't I hear that Knight Ops was deep in their own shit in Mississippi while we were raiding that warehouse?"

Downs nodded. "It's clear that two teams are essential. I promise to fight for you, Sullivan."

"'Preciate it, sir. If you don't mind, I'm dragging ass and could use a hot shower and some sleep."

"Get somebody to take care of that cut over your eye too."

He nodded, thinking of Nevaeh standing between his legs and his hands exploring the soft flesh of her waist as she tended to the cut that had been put there by a board with lethal nails. He'd come close to losing an eye, but he'd made damn sure the man who'd delivered that blow hadn't gotten up again.

He heaved himself to his feet and offered Downs a smile. "Thank you, sir." What he didn't say was he appreciated the camaraderie of their talk as much as getting things off his chest.

They shook hands, and Nash took his leave. When he walked out into the parking lot, he found all his team, looking as worn as he felt but casually standing around talking.

"Don't you assholes have homes to go to?" he drawled out.

197

Woody, who was leaning against Nash's Jeep, straightened away to clasp hands with Nash. "I'm heading off. Just wanted to make sure you jerks were stable."

Jess barked out a laugh. "I'd like to meet a man who does this shit for a living who's stable. We're all fucking crazy or we wouldn't be here." He clapped Nash and Woody on the shoulders and then headed across the parking lot to his old pickup only a true Southern boy would drive.

Nash said goodbye to the others and then climbed into his Jeep. Fatigue hit him like a brick wall, but he rolled down the window and enjoyed the breeze on his face as he drove to Nevaeh's house.

He hoped she was home—he hadn't bothered to text. He didn't totally know her habits, but he intended to start learning as of right now.

When he arrived, he cut the engine and sat there a second, looking toward the house. But what he saw was a man who'd been haunting his dreams.

Adrenaline hit his system, and he jerked open his door, striding across the street to intercept the man.

"Antonio." He scoped out everything around him for half a block. If Antonio had brought his men with him here to the States, it would spell danger for Nevaeh and her family, and Nash wasn't letting that happen.

Before Antonio had taken two steps, Nash had him by the shoulder in a firm grip. "What the hell are you doin' here?"

Antonio threw him a look, revealing the creases drawn across his face from years of rough living. "Am I being taken in or something? I didn't do anything wrong."

"We both know I can't let you walk in that house without interrogating you first. Come with me." He took the man to his Jeep and pushed him inside. Then he drove.

"Start talkin'," he demanded.

Antonio sat next to him, curled forward slightly, his shoulders hunched. "I wanted to leave with you and your men. But I couldn't just then."

"You're speaking in Spanish, man. Do you realize that?"

Antonio threw him a glance of surprise. "It's been a long time since I spoke English," he said carefully around the words that were now foreign to him.

Nash parked in a lot at the far end, so they were well away from the shoppers coming in and out. He kept a firm eye on the man seated next to him. He didn't trust him any more than he had the men who'd kidnapped and held him captive. To Nash's thinking, Antonio had been indoctrinated and was no longer the man they hoped he would be.

"Who came with you to Texas?" he asked.

He sliced his gaze from Nash's. "I came alone."

199

Nash wasn't standing for this bullshit. He was tired, hungry and he wanted his girl. Besides, he couldn't tolerate a fucking liar.

He slammed his hand off the dash, making Antonio leap in his seat. "Goddammit, tell me the truth! Who did you come with? Was it Lopez? One of his men?" Nash had dealt with the regrets of not taking out every fucking person in that operation.

He shook his head. "N-no. It's a woman. Her name is Alicia. She was one of Lopez's—well, under his rule. He brought her in to"—he fisted his hands before going on— "service us men, to keep us quiet and happy, understand?"

Glancing at Nash again, his eyes flared with fury. A fury Nash hadn't totally understood before he'd met Nevaeh.

It was the look a man got when he would move hell and earth to protect the woman he loved.

Fuck, Nash loved Nevaeh.

He barely had a chance to register the thought before Antonio continued.

"She was more than that to me, and we became close. I had to go back for her." He lifted his eyes to Nash's. "She's carrying my baby."

Nash was speechless for a moment. He nodded. "Where is she now?"

"At a hotel. We made off with enough money to keep us for a week or two before I could get a job, in case my family doesn't want to help us. I understand if they don't."

"I think you underestimate your place in your family, even after all these years."

His words broke down something inside Antonio. He lowered his head and tears began to drip onto his lap. "It wasn't as Lopez told me then."

Jesus, the man had brainwashed Antonio.

"I can get you the counseling you need. You and your woman both."

He nodded.

"Will he come for you?"

Antonio understood what he was asking. "I don't know. I have a lot of information." He tapped his temple. "In here."

"Then he'll come after you. But I can put a stop to that. Look, I'm going to have to put guards around you and your woman until this shit's over. But I can't have you around your parents or Nevaeh until it's all clear."

Antonio let out a sigh of a man with far more weight on his shoulders than anybody of his age should be bearing. "I understand what you're saying, but I'd like to see my family before that happens. Is that okay?"

It went against Nash's initial instincts, though he could see where Antonio was coming from.

"Only if I'm there too."

"Were you following me? Is that how you found me?"

"No. I was coming to see Nevaeh."

His face blanked.

"Your sister and I are seeing each other."

"Did she send you then, to find me?"

"It's an involved story, but one I'll tell you later. For now, let's see about this family reunion and then I'll ensure you and your lady friend are safe and guarded. Has she had any medical care during her pregnancy?"

"There was no way to get it. Nobody knew she was carrying my child either. They all believed it was a bastard. But Alicia's no whore."

"I believe you." Nash put the Jeep in drive, his mind jumping ahead to what would happen when he showed up on Nevaeh's doorstep with her long, lost brother.

* * * * *

Nevaeh stepped from the shower and reached for a fluffy towel. As she dried her body and hair, it was impossible not to think of the man she wanted touching both. His hands all over her, his mouth on hers.

Her movements slowed automatically with her thoughts, and long minutes later, she squeezed the water from her hair and wrapped her hair in the towel.

The light robe she slipped into felt like the most decadent caress against her hungry, too-hot flesh. She needed Nash. The support and comfort he offered while he was near had given her — at last — the ability to release her tight rein on control.

Because of it, she felt so light and free, like she was ready to take on the world.

Even if it was just telling Nash how she felt.

It's too soon.

But if she'd learned anything in her life, it was that you couldn't tell people enough that you loved them.

With Nash and his dangerous line of work, who knew what could befall him. Even strong heroes fell...

She couldn't think about that. Next time she saw him, she'd find the right moment to say what was in her heart.

She opened the bathroom door and released the cloud of steam into the hallway. As soon as she took one step out onto the cool tile floor, a scream brought her up short. Not any scream — a shrill scream that curdled her blood.

"Momma!" She took off, following the sound, and when she rushed into the living room, she let out a cry of her own.

"Antonio!" She felt her knees start to quake, but Nash was there too and he dragged her up against his chest, anchoring her. After so many years, her brother was standing in their living room, with his arms around their mother.

She had to get in on that hug. Squeezing Nash's arm, she gave him a glance. He nodded and released her.

The few steps to reach her family was too many and when she gripped at Antonio's shirt, he turned to her. Tears streaked his face, and she let out a laugh of joy as she put her arms around her brother.

He was thinner, sinewy. He was not the same young man who'd left this house, but it didn't matter, because he wasn't only alive but back with them. How?

She had to put the question to Nash.

Her mother shook with the shock of it all, and Antonio seemed to be the only thing holding her up. Nevaeh slipped her arm around her mother's back too, and together they sucked in the moment.

"You've grown up," her brother said to her.

Nevaeh laughed again. How good that felt. "That happens to kids." Her cheeks were beginning to ache from how wide her smile was. "We have to call Dad!"

Hearing this, her mother got flustered, waving her hands. "Get me my phone! Somebody tell him to come home at once!"

"Where is he?" Nash asked, stepping toward them.

Nevaeh tilted her head to meet his gaze. "You're bleeding."

He shrugged. "I'll take care of it later. This is more important."

In his eyes, she saw the warmth anybody would after watching this reunion. "My father ran down to a buddy's to watch the game."

"Where's your phone? I'll use it to call since it has the contact in it." Nash dropped his stare over her attire, which was her flimsy robe and the towel on her head. She felt the stroke of his eyes over her skin. "Still on the bathroom sink."

"I'll get it." He looked as if he wanted to take her into the bathroom, shut the door and have his way with her. But he did nothing more than give her a quirk of his lips. "Stay here with your family. I'll bring your dad home."

She nodded, growing warmer with happiness at how amazing and helpful Nash had been to her — her family. His spot in her heart had been there almost from the start, and now it was taking over, twining around the body part until there was no place left to go but burrow into her soul.

She was fine with that.

Antonio drew their mother to the sofa and made her sit. Then he crowded close to her, and Nevaeh took up the other side. Her mother was talking to him rapidly, firing questions about his health and wellbeing, was he safe and so on. Antonio answered them in a low, calm voice while Nevaeh and her mother took it all in.

Nash drifted back into the room, catching her eye. She offered him a big smile and was rewarded with a wink. That gesture had her highly aware of her undressed state.

The towel atop her head wobbled, and she pulled it off. He watched her with heavy-lidded eyes.

"I don't want to miss any of this, but I'll be right back." She got off the sofa, and holding the towel in her hands, made her way toward her room. On the way past Nash, she grabbed him by the arm and dragged him with her.

Not that she had to do much dragging—the man seemed more than eager to get her alone.

As soon as she entered her room, she turned to him. He spun his arms around her and pulled her onto tiptoe, crushing his mouth over hers. A moan of desire left her, but now was not the time. Still, she couldn't resist kissing him back.

When things began to get too heated, he withdrew. "I'm sorry. I shouldn't be ravishing you. I shouldn't want to push you down on that bed and sink my cock into your pussy, which I know is bare beneath this itty bitty bit of cloth." He ran his hand over her spine, hitching the robe too high so her cheeks were exposed.

She shivered. "We need to spend time together. But first, this—"

"Is about family," he finished with a nod.

"Yes. I'll just get dressed."

"Go ahead. I'll watch."

She smacked at him and turned him to the door. "My momma can't afford so many shocks in one day. Go out and wait for me."

He threaded his fingers into the wet, tangled hair over her ear. "You're gorgeous. And I'll do anything you ask of me... except walk away." His dark eyes drilled into her with complete sincerity.

"Nash." His name hitched in her throat. "I won't be asking that of you."

"Good." He gave a nod.

"Why don't you let me tend to that cut?"

"I'm good." He grinned and left her room.

It took her seconds to throw on shorts and a T-shirt and brush her hair but much longer to get that look he'd sent her way out of her mind. Why would he ever believe she'd ask him to walk away? They needed to have that talk, clearly soon.

When she stepped into the living room again, she had to delight in the sight of her brother. He and their mother had their arms around each other. When they spotted her, they held out their arms to draw her in too. Then their father came through the door, and the reunion took on a whole other level of emotion as father and son set eyes on each other after a decade.

Nevaeh saw Nash slip out the door and ran outside onto the stoop. "Nash!"

He hadn't left the porch but was standing like a sentry before the door, scanning the neighborhood.

He turned to her. "Darlin', it's okay. I'm just checking things out."

A shudder ran over her. "Is he still in danger?"

He didn't need to say so—she was coming to know his expressions better than he probably wanted. A man like Nash was good at keeping everything set behind a mask, but Nevaeh looked at him with not only her eyes but her heart.

Reaching up, she cupped his jaw. The scruff of beard rasping against her fingers had her nipples tightening and her stomach clenching, low. "Thank you for everything you've done for us, Nash."

His throat moved. "I hope you know it's more than just duty that has me sticking around."

Her heart gave a leap. She ran her thumb over his jaw and up to the corner of his lips. She started to speak, but he stopped her. "Shh. Go back inside. There's plenty of time for us, but right now it's about your brother." He squeezed her shoulders and turned her back to the door.

Inside, while she sat and listened to Antonio's tale alongside her parents, she realized just what Nash had really done—and continued to. He'd changed not only her and her parents' lives but Antonio's. After so many years in Mexico, her brother had stopped hoping. But Nash had plowed onto the scene and given him the means and desire to escape.

And Antonio had done exactly that with the woman he loved, the woman who was carrying his child.

When they all heard this news, their mother broke down all over again, and their father looked about to get up and dance a jig around the room. "This news alone is worth missing all the games this season for!"

Antonio laughed. A haunted look still clung to him, and Nevaeh knew that would take some time to dissipate. She would help him in any way possible, and his loved one too. He promised to bring her here first thing in the morning and assured them she was safe, tucked in at a hotel in a bed finer than any she'd ever known.

After long hours of talk, Nevaeh got up and went outside again. Sure enough, Nash was still here, their personal special ops protector.

His gaze landed on her face. In the faint glow from the streetlights, she made out a smile curving his lips at one corner. "You're happy," he stated.

She nodded, throat closing off for a brief moment. "So happy, Nash. You can't imagine."

He searched her face. "I think I can."

Again, her heart juddered in her chest at his words.

The timing couldn't get any more perfect.

Stepping up close, she eased her arms around his neck. He bent over her, filling her nose with his masculine scent. "Nash..." She breathed out his name.

He dropped his forehead to hers. "Darlin'." His throat clicked as he swallowed. "There's something I want to tell you."

"I want to talk to you too."

He nuzzled her nose with his own. "You're so damn perfect in my arms. I can't imagine ever holding anybody else like this."

She went still, just listening to the croon of his low voice as he said all the things a woman longed to hear when it came to the man she loved.

"Nash, I know we came together in an odd way. Under extreme circumstances."

"Yes. But that doesn't mean what I feel isn't real. It is, darlin'. Nevaeh," he said with a new urgency, "I love you. You have driven me to the brink of insanity with wanting you—and not just your body." As if defying his words, his hands slithered over her waist to cup her backside. Desire spiked through her pussy.

"Nash, I can't believe you beat me to telling you!"

"Telling me what?"

"That I love you. That I know it has happened quickly, but the things I'm feeling I don't want to end."

Emotions cut across his shadowed features. Then he shook his head as if in disbelief. "You came out here to tell me you love me?"

She nodded — and then punched his arm, making him laugh.

"I didn't know this was a competition, but if it is, I'm glad to have said the words first."

She cuddled closer to him. "Why is that?"

"Because I don't want you to ever think I was pushed into just saying it back. I love you, woman, and I'm never going to stop."

She yanked his head down and kissed him. The soft brushing of lips turned to a bruising, carnal demand that had them both shaking with need after only a few seconds.

With a forefinger, he found the undercurve of her ass in her shorts and strummed nerve endings she didn't know she had. "God, I fucking want you. If this wasn't your parents' house, I'd pin you to this wall with my cock buried inside you."

Her pussy flooded at the promise of his dirty talk. When they finally got alone and the timing was right, she knew this was going to be one hell of an explosion between the two of them.

She just hoped he didn't get called away before she could strip down his big, hard body and run her hands — and tongue — all over every muscle he owned.

Chapter Eleven

Nash folded his arms and stared out between the tiny cracks in the blinds. Behind him, the men at the table were completely silent as their task ahead weighed on them.

How could it not? Nevaeh's brother might be back on US soil, but he was far from safe. Lopez and his thugs were not going to give him up so easily

"What are you thinkin', Sully?" Woody's voice came to him.

He turned and stared at the five of them. "I think we fucked up by leaving even a single person alive. The mission was to get Vincent out at any cost. My mistake was backing down, but sometimes you can't escape killing and it has nothing to do with anger management. When it comes to this team, we don't back down. Ever."

"It's the Texas Ranger in you," Woody said, looking at his own capable fingers spread on the table. "You can't help but spare lives when possible."

"Yeah, but now we're Ranger Ops. We were chosen, because OFFSUS saw something ruthless enough in us to get shit done. We failed to get shit done, and that's on me. But it's ending right now too."

Woody looked up. All eyes fixed on Nash. "Does that mean we're vacationing in Mexico again, boss man?"

He gave a hard nod. "That's exactly what this means. They're going to keep coming for us. This time, we need to rack up the body count, because loyalty is how those guys operate. If one dies, the next in line picks up the battle sword, and we aren't going to allow that to happen."

"I'm with ya, Sully. Point me in the right direction." Cavanagh stood, elongating to his full height of six-four. The expression on his face was just what Nash wanted to see—that hungry, take-no-prisoners look that would get the job done.

Everyone else stood, forming a solidarity that had pride swimming in Nash's veins.

"We roll out in an hour. Pack light, because we'll be heavy on the ammo."

As the guys disbursed to collect their gear, Nash turned to the window again. The slits he could see through didn't show him the scope of the world, but he had a good enough idea of what was going on out there that a view wasn't necessary.

It wasn't as if he had given up watching Lopez after leaving Mexico. No, he had all the intel he needed to make this mission a go—those guys were coming for Vincent, and this time they didn't have slavery on the mind. They wanted him and everyone he loved dead. The old way was to kill everyone, scourge the bloodline.

Well, Nash intended to take it further and wipe out everyone associated with those fuckers, and he'd personally escort them to hell's gates with a smile on his face.

Soon enough, he told himself. Right now, he had the issue of Nevaeh on his mind. He hadn't been able to spend enough time with her, and he was feeling that separation like a blow. This was how it would always be for them—him handling his business and Ranger Ops always coming first.

He had to do something to show her how he felt.

A minute later, he was on the phone with a florist, having half a dozen roses delivered to her house. It's wasn't fucking near enough, but it was a start. If this was going to be the norm, he'd better find a florist with better prices or he wouldn't be able to afford rent.

After he finished the transaction, he called Nevaeh. She answered on the second ring, her voice a little breathless.

"Were you running?" he asked as soon as she picked up.

"No."

"You sound a little out of breath."

She was silent a moment. "Just happy to hear from you."

All their unfinished kisses slammed into his mind, and he found himself growing hard at the thought of her. Dammit, he wanted her.

"Nevaeh, darlin', I'm sorry. I have to go away a while."

"How long is a while?"

"Hopefully not long."

Silence again. He tightened his lips.

"Nash." Her voice came out as a whisper.

"Yeah, darlin'?"

"Say it to me. Tell me."

His heart filled his throat, and he pinched the bridge of his nose. "I love you, Nevaeh. And I'll come back to you."

Those must have been the right words, because he heard her let out a breath. "I believe you. And I love you."

He smiled, shaking his head lightly in wonder. How had he come to this place in his life? Sure, it was early times in their relationship—hell, it was like a balloon just getting wind beneath it to sail into the sky. And times like these would make it tougher. In the end, they'd reach new heights together and then look back on this moment and be proud of fighting for what they believed in.

They both believed in a *them*.

* * * * *

Nevaeh sat at her desk, a fingertip pressed to her lips as she stared at the cubicle wall before her. A few family photos were scattered there. Until recently, she hadn't been able to place one of her brother there, but this morning she had printed one off her phone of him standing with their parents and pinned it to her wall.

Staring at it, she just knew where Nash was headed. The fact that Antonio and his girlfriend were being protected and not allowed to leave their guarded hotel room besides that single visit together to the Vincents' home said it all.

Ranger Ops had taken off for Mexico to end it.

A shiver of emotion ran through her—part fear and part arousal that her man could take care of business this way.

She hadn't spoken to him in two days now, but that was normal, right? He couldn't very well call her in the thick of it. The extravagant roses filling her bedroom were his way of telling her he was still thinking of her, and that would have to be enough for now.

"Nevaeh, some files for you."

She turned at the sound of the voice that was very out of place in this office.

Prickles of happiness washed over her skin, and she leaped up, hurling herself at the man holding out yet another bouquet.

"Oh my God!" She looped her arms around Nash's neck and clung to him, inhaling his scent and reveling in the feel of his big body against hers.

He brought his arms around her, lowering his face to her hair. "I never knew you'd be so happy to have some files."

She giggled and pulled back to look him over.

He wasn't harmed, was her first thought. But a deeper look into his eyes told her that he'd seen and done things that were still haunting him.

Pulling one arm free of his neck, she laced her fingers with his. The calluses on his hand were enough to send a shock of need through her.

His gaze intensified.

"Let me tell my boss I'm taking some sick time."

His mouth twisted. "I'll wait outside."

She couldn't get out the door fast enough. As soon as she got into the open air, Nash grabbed her up and kissed her — right there outside her office building, and she didn't care who saw.

She angled her head and kissed him back with all the yearning burning inside of her.

"Will you come home with me?" he asked, low.

The rumble sent new shocks of want into her belly.

"Nothing could hold me back," she answered in that same breathy tone she'd answered his phone call with the other day.

He took her hand and led her to his Jeep, opening the door for her and settling her inside before he walked around the vehicle and jumped behind the wheel.

When he placed his heavy hand on her thigh, she wiggled in her seat. He shot her a look. "You want me. I can see your hard nipples through your top."

She didn't bother to cover the evidence, not a bit embarrassed by what had given her away. To prove this, she reached up and unfastened the top two buttons of her blouse, showing him a healthy amount of cleavage.

He could barely keep his eyes on the road. "Damn." He pulled his head away from her leg to adjust his cock. Then he reached over and dipped two fingers into her cleavage. Before she could arch into his touch, one long finger swiped into her bra cup, right over her taut nipple.

She cried out, and he strummed his finger back and forth over the bud that was growing hard enough to throb.

"How far is your place?"

He chuckled. "Eager?"

Instead of answering, she reached over and cupped his hard cock. He stretched his hips upward and groaned. She molded the cloth of his pants to his arousal, learning the ridges right up to the mushroomed tip, barely harnessed behind his fly.

218

"Three blocks," he ground out. "You keep that up and I might not make it that far."

"What will you do?" she asked with a coy tilt of her head.

His dark eyes raked over her. "Pull over and throw you into the back seat."

She laughed, feeling more carefree than she had in her life. She had everything she wanted, at last. Thanks to Nash, her family was whole. And she had the man himself to love on her entire life.

When they arrived in front of a small bungalow cut in between several larger houses, she could hardly hold back her excitement. Being alone with him, naked, rolling in his sheets... She wanted it with a fire she didn't know possible until now.

He parked swiftly and got out, taking her by the hand and towing her fast up the paver sidewalk.

"How do you have time to mow your grass?" she asked as she was shuttled to the door.

"I don't. I hire the kid next door. Is that really what's on your mind right this minute?" He tossed a look her way that was a flame licking over her skin.

"No. The burning question in my mind is how long can you hold out while I suck your cock?"

His chest inflated but he made no sound, only unlocked his door and hauled her inside. She didn't even get a peek at the interior before he spun her, flattening her against the closed door with her arms pinned over her head.

His rough hold on her wrists only raised her need another notch. She tipped her face up, and he swooped in to kiss her. The plunges of his tongue had her panties flooding with arousal, and she wriggled wantonly against his muscles.

"You want to know how long I can last if you suck my cock?" he murmured between nibbles of her lips and sweeping passes with his tongue.

Had she said that? Her mind was a blank to anything but what was going on this very moment. She whimpered, "Uhh."

"Let me tell you, darlin', it isn't very fucking long. These lips…" He kissed her hard. "Wrapped around my length…" He bit her lower lip, dragging her nearer. "Will be my undoing."

She worked her hands free of his grasp and set them on his chest. Looking into his eyes, she said, "Take me to bed. I want to see for myself."

With a grunt of amusement, he lifted her off her feet, her legs dangling over his brick-hard forearm as he stormed through his small house. The living room was a blur, but she could see it later—right now, she only had eyes for Nash.

He kicked open the bedroom door and crossed to a bed. The scents of his musk and fresh laundry rose around her as he lowered her to the mattress. He followed her down, pressing her thighs apart to make room for his broad body.

When his hard cock edged against her needy pussy, she moaned.

"My question is how long can you last if I tongue your wet pussy?" he rumbled.

"Seconds," she responded, pulling him down.

They tore at each other's clothes, and he thrust a finger into her pussy. She clenched around him, breathing hard against the need to come from just one single touch.

"Sixty-nine me," she gritted out.

He froze, and she felt him shudder against her. "Hell."

"I want to taste you and you want to taste me." She pushed on his shoulders, and to her delight, he acquiesced, moving onto the mattress and placing her over him with her liquid heat centered over his lips. She moaned at the sight of his beautiful, rigid cock rising up to meet her lips.

She opened her mouth, closed her eyes and swallowed him right to the root.

* * * * *

The exquisite heat and pressure of Nevaeh's mouth around him had Nash shaking to hold back. To distract himself, he parted her folds with his thumbs and slipped his tongue into her soaking pussy.

Juices wet his lips and brought a growl to his throat. She wiggled her gorgeous backside downward to get closer, and he took the chance to sink two fingers into her body even as he sucked her clit into his mouth.

The soft pulls of his lips had her moaning in seconds, and her pussy walls tightened and released rhythmically around his fingers. He pushed them up higher, feeling the soft, spongy inner wall. In seconds, she was going wild, bucking into him as she sucked him harder.

When she cupped his balls in one soft, warm hand, lashing them upward to stroke the sensitive spot beneath them, he just about unloaded in her mouth.

Mentally biting back his need to blow, he doubled his efforts, curling his fingers to stroke her G-spot. Batting her clit with his tongue wasn't enough—he tongued it hard and fast.

She stiffened and shook in his hold. The instant she let go, he finger-fucked her hard, banging her until the final pulse of her orgasm had her cooing out his name.

He flipped her into the mattress and hovered over her, staring into her eyes. The windows of stained glass showed him every bit of her soul, and there he saw the force of her love for him.

"Christ, I love you, woman." He gripped his dick at the base and guided it between her legs. When he plunged into her, she wrapped her arms and legs around him, riding with him.

The bed shook with the strength of their movements. Her love words fell on his ears and her nails scored his back, the sting wiping away the memories of what he'd just done in Mexico. He hoped to hell his men were getting the same release from their ghosts too.

Then Nevaeh started to thrash beneath him, and he felt how close she was.

He was instantly on the border of his own release, edging between pain of holding back and pleasure so intense that he didn't know if he'd survive it.

When she slid her hand around his nape and yanked him in for a kiss, she came — and he let go.

Tumbling over and over as jets of cum filled her pussy.

Long seconds passed where all he heard was their breathing.

She smoothed a hand down his spine, and he winced as she hit the place a bullet had grazed him. Woody had patched him up, and he wore a clean bandage.

"Oh my God, you're hurt!"

He held his cock deep inside her, looking into her eyes. "Not bad."

"A knife wound?"

"Bullet. Lucky I moved sideways and it only glanced over me."

Her mouth opened in a wide O. "Nash Sullivan! Why didn't you tell me?"

"Why? Would you have kept me from giving you all those delicious orgasms?" He bent to nibble her lips again.

"I... I... I don't know!"

He rolled off, drawing her with him. When she was in his arms, he could talk to her freely. "Darlin', things happen. It's part of the job."

"What if it was me coming home with a bullet wound?"

"That's different."

"How?"

"Because it isn't your job." He kissed the crease between her brows gently. He had to ask the question he'd been fearing for days now, ever since he'd realized how tough his leaving constantly could be on her.

"Nevaeh, can you handle it? Being with a man like me?"

She was still in his hold for so long that he began to worry. When he was about to say more, to tell her that he understood and even though he didn't want to contemplate it, he'd let her walk away, she spoke.

"Nash, I can't handle *not* being with you. It will take some getting used to, but... I can do it. For love."

Warmth spread over his heart, and he pulled her in to kiss her mouth. The tenderness between them was the thing that would continue to ground him again and again, no matter what the fuck happened in Ranger Ops.

"Good, because I need you," he grated out.

She kissed him again and when she pulled back, her eyes were twinkling with mischief. "All those flowers you sent made up for a lot."

He barked a surprised laugh. "I see how you operate now. If that's what it takes, then I'll open an account at the florist's."

She clutched him closer and hitched her thigh over his hip, grinding her wetness against him insinuatingly. "Just always promise you'll come home to me."

"Always." He sealed the deal by drawing her overtop him and sliding inside her in one slick glide.

All her thick hair fell around him, and she began to move.

Epilogue

Crash after crash exploded in Nevaeh's ears, and the big Ranger Ops men surrounding her high-fived all around.

Nevaeh looked up at the scoreboard. X after X stood out on each of the lines of the bowling scorecard, while her name only boasted a single spare. Clearly, she needed to get much better at bowling if she was going to walk away with any dignity in the future.

"Beers all around." Woody returned carrying a six-pack and an extra wine spritzer for her. He handed it to her with a smile, and she returned it.

None of the guys seemed remotely surprised when Nash had informed them he and Nevaeh were seeing each other, and they'd invited her to their weekly bowling parties with warm welcomes.

"You remembered what I like," Nevaeh said as she took the bottle with thanks.

Woody tapped his temple with a fingertip. "My job to remember things."

Judging by the look of him lately, he was remembering—a bit too much. She'd mentioned it to Nash, but he'd only told her he'd talk to his buddy.

Whatever he'd said, though, didn't seem to be helping, and she'd caught each of the guys sending Woody worried looks now and then over the course of the past few months.

Nash came over to get his beer. When he drew near to Nevaeh, he tugged on her long braid hanging down her spine and leaned in to whisper in her ear. "He'll be all right."

She curled her hand up around his jaw. "You sure?"

He nodded, rubbing his beard stubble against her cheek.

Nevaeh believed him. After all, Nash had recognized the need for counseling for Antonio and his wife. And the pair was working through their adjustment into a new life together in a rental home not far away from where her parents lived. Which was good, because her parents had not taken her moving out very well.

She and Nash made sure to visit as often as possible, bringing the whole family together.

Woody straightened, staring past them. She and Nash pivoted to look and saw another Sullivan man sauntering their way, a shit-eating grin on his face.

"Penn!" She jumped up, and Nash reached him in a few steps, pulling him into a bro-hug.

The guys all added their greetings with similar thumps on the back or fist-bumps. Then Nash gave Penn his beer and went to get more in celebration.

Penn looked at Nevaeh, a smile on his face. "I knew it. A well-loved woman."

She flushed hotly and slid her gaze to her man, standing at the counter making his purchase. Then Nash turned and caught her eye, giving her a wide grin that had her insides fluttering.

She raised her bottle to Penn, and he clinked his against it. "Yes, a well-loved woman."

THE END

Author's Note: If you've enjoyed this book, please leave a review! They make authors happy!

READ ON for a sneak peek at Within Range, book 2 of Ranger Ops series!

Em Petrova

Em Petrova was raised by hippies in the wilds of Pennsylvania but told her parents at the age of four she wanted to be a gypsy when she grew up. She has a soft spot for babies, puppies and 90s Grunge music and believes in Bigfoot and aliens. She started writing at the age of twelve and prides herself on making her characters larger than life and her sex scenes hotter than hot.

She burst into the world of publishing in 2010 after having five beautiful bambinos and figuring they were old enough to get their own snacks while she pounds away at the keys. In her not-so-spare time, she is fur-mommy to a Labradoodle named Daisy Hasselhoff.

Find More Books by Em Petrova Em Petrova

Em Petrova was raised by hippies in the wilds of Pennsylvania but told her parents at the age of four she wanted to be a gypsy when she grew up. She has a soft spot for babies, puppies and 90s Grunge music and believes in Bigfoot and aliens. She started writing at the age of twelve and prides herself on making her characters larger than life and her sex scenes hotter than hot.

She burst into the world of publishing in 2010 after having five beautiful bambinos and figuring they were old enough to get their own snacks while she pounds away at the keys. In her not-so-spare time, she is fur-mommy to a Labradoodle named Daisy Hasselhoff and works as editor with USA Today and New York Times bestselling authors.

Find Em Petrova at empetrova.com

Other Titles by Em Petrova

Ranger Ops
AT CLOSE RANGE
WITHIN RANGE
POINT BLANK RANGE

Knight Ops Series
ALL KNIGHTER
HEAT OF THE KNIGHT

HOT LOUISIANA KNIGHT
AFTER MIDKNIGHT
KNIGHT SHIFT
ANGEL OF THE KNIGHT
O CHRISTMAS KNIGHT

Wild West Series
SOMETHING ABOUT A LAWMAN
SOMETHING ABOUT A SHERIFF
SOMETHING ABOUT A BOUNTY HUNTER
SOMETHING ABOUT A MOUNTAIN MAN

Operation Cowboy Series
KICKIN' UP DUST
SPURS AND SURRENDER

The Boot Knockers Ranch Series
PUSHIN' BUTTONS
BODY LANGUAGE
REINING MEN
ROPIN' HEARTS
ROPE BURN
COWBOY NOT INCLUDED

The Boot Knockers Ranch Montana
COWBOY BY CANDLELIGHT

THE BOOT KNOCKER'S BABY
ROPIN' A ROMEO

Country Fever Series
HARD RIDIN'
LIP LOCK
UNBROKEN
SOMETHIN' DIRTY

Rope 'n Ride Series
BUCK
RYDER
RIDGE
WEST
LANE
WYNONNA

Rope 'n Ride On Series
JINGLE BOOTS
DOUBLE DIPPIN
LICKS AND PROMISES
A COWBOY FOR CHRISTMAS
LIPSTICK 'N LEAD

The Dalton Boys

COWBOY CRAZY Hank's story
COWBOY BARGAIN Cash's story
COWBOY CRUSHIN' Witt's story
COWBOY SECRET Beck's story
COWBOY RUSH Kade's Story
COWBOY MISTLETOE a Christmas novella
COWBOY FLIRTATION Ford's story
COWBOY TEMPTATION Easton's story
COWBOY SURPRISE Justus's story

Single Titles and Boxes
STRANDED AND STRADDLED
LASSO MY HEART
SINFUL HEARTS
BLOWN DOWN
FALLEN
FEVERED HEARTS
WRONG SIDE OF LOVE

Club Ties Series
LOVE TIES
HEART TIES
MARKED AS HIS
SOUL TIES
ACE'S WILD

Firehouse 5 Series
ONE FIERY NIGHT
CONTROLLED BURN
SMOLDERING HEARTS

The Quick and the Hot Series
DALLAS NIGHTS
SLICK RIDER
SPURRED ON

READ ON for a sneak peek of <u>WITHIN RANGE</u>!

Two years ago

"Are you gonna stand here and let this happen?"

Shaw's father gave him the sideways look that meant he'd better fix his disposition and do it fucking fast.

He tugged at the collar of his dress shirt. It felt uncomfortably tighter with each second that counted down to the wedding ceremony.

"What are you talking about?" Shaw shot back. But he knew—and playing stupid wasn't going to fix the situation. The woman he loved was walking down that aisle, and it wasn't to him.

His father squared up with him. Lawdy, this situation was going downhill like a pig in a mudslide. His father looked him in the eyes, and his voice came out low and intense.

"You love that woman. Why the hell are you letting this happen? You don't get many chances at happiness in this life, son."

Shaw stared over his father's shoulder toward the altar, where his buddy John stood alongside his brother as best man, suited up and waiting for the first strains of the wedding march.

Without looking at his father, Shaw muttered, "I can't just stop the wedding."

"So you're going to stop your life instead?"

The words struck Shaw like a hail of bullets, each finding its mark deep within him.

Goddammit.

He turned from his father.

His black leather dress shoes tapped out a beat on the floor that mirrored his heart. Stained glass flashed by his vision and he stepped through a doorway into the bridal suite.

A gasp sounded as Atalee's female entourage saw him standing in the doorway, but he couldn't see a fucking thing but the bride in white, her honey blonde hair piled in an extravagant updo with little fucking flowers tucked into the strands and a floor-length veil.

Dammit.

"I need to speak to Atalee alone," he grated out.

Her eyes found his, big and chocolate brown, the depths filled with surprise.

He was about to surprise her even more, and with any luck, three hundred wedding guests when she cancelled her wedding and ran away with Shaw.

The bride's mother touched her arm, and she gave her a nod and smile. The women scuttled past Shaw, and he threw a glance over his shoulder to ensure they wouldn't overhear what he was about to say.

As he moved toward the most gorgeous woman he'd ever seen in his life, his throat dried out. He swallowed hard and stepped up before her.

"Atalee..."

With her face tilted up to his and wearing all white, his heart threatened to give out from pounding so hard.

Kiss your bride.

She's somebody else's bride.

Dammit to hell.

"What is it, Shaw? Is something wrong?" Her soft-spoken manner took hold of him by the balls. This woman owned him, pure and simple.

He grabbed her hands, hovering over her. Emotion threatened to close off his throat, but he wasn't a quitter or a coward. He was a fucking Texas Ranger, and he wanted this woman with every cell of his being.

"Atalee, you can't marry Johnny."

She blinked up at him and paled slightly. "What happened? Did he back out?"

"No, no, nothing like that," he rushed to say before she lost more color from her face. His heart flexed hard, painfully. "Atalee, I've known you for years now."

Confusion creased her blonde brows. "Yes."

He was fucking this all up. *Just say it,* he ordered himself.

"I can't let you walk down that aisle and marry Johnny, because I'm in love with you."

A beat of silence followed, and her baby browns widened.

"Baby doll, I can give you everything you ever wanted. I'm better for you than the man out there." He gestured toward the main part of the church where all her guests were expecting her.

She dropped her head and stared at the bouquet she held. The petals of the brightly-colored flowers trembled in her shaking hands.

"Shaw, why are you saying these things to me?"

"Because I can't let you marry another man without telling you how I feel. I can't watch you destroy your life with someone who won't love you the way I do."

She took a step back and then another. His instinct was to grab her back, yank her flush to his body and kiss her with all the passion flowing inside him. Three long years he'd wanted her. Johnny had been his friend for much longer. They'd trained together as Texas State Troopers, but only Nash had gone on to be a Texas Ranger. All the while, Atalee had been achieving her psychiatry degree and had started on her master's.

His chest inflated as he gathered wind to speak, to somehow convince her to walk away with him.

"Atalee, listen—"

Her face twisted in a grimace of pain. "No, you listen, Shaw Woodward. You can't just walk in here and tell me you love me minutes before I'm about to marry your friend. Hear those words? *Your friend.* What kind of man betrays a buddy like this?"

"I don't care about that. All I want is you."

She took another step away from him. He was losing her. Lifting the bouquet like a ward against evil spirits, she glared at him. "Get out of here and don't come back, Shaw. I'm marrying Johnny. I *love* Johnny."

Jesus Christ, those words hurt.

Shaw wasn't known for giving up easy, though. In two steps he was with her, a hand planted on her lower back as he jerked her against him. Slamming his mouth over all that lipstick that another man was meant to kiss off her sweet, honeyed lips. For a moment, she stood still in his hold.

Then she melted.

Just a bit.

It was enough for him to sweep his tongue through her mouth, gathering all the flavors he knew were it for him for the rest of his life.

Till death did they part.

Suddenly, she shoved her hands against him. Flower petals crushed against his suit jacket and tumbled to the floor as she stumbled back.

"Damn you, Shaw! Leave!"

He felt his jaw muscles bunch up and knew he was getting pissed. He leveled his gaze at her. "You sure you want that? Because you felt yourself melt into my kiss just as much as I did."

"Fuck you!" She came at him, bouquet flopping in her hand on smashed stems. She hit him square in the chest, but he didn't even rock on his feet. She was an itty-bitty thing and he was six-two. Who knew seeing hatred on a woman's face could bring a man to his knees?

She was fucking killing him.

"Get out of here! I never want to see you again."

He firmed his jaw and just stared at her for a heavy heartbeat. Her chest rose and fell with fury, but all he saw was the woman he wanted through thick and thin. It might be their first fight and later they'd laugh about it.

"I don't have feelings for you, Shaw, and I never will. Now go." Her eyes narrowed to slits, and her words were venom darts, striking him one by lethal one.

He brought a fist to his lips, pressing back any words that he might say to ruin her life even more than he already had. In the end, he gave a nod, sent her one last look that would have to suffice for the rest of his days and walked out.

On the way to the front doors, he walked past his father, who caught him by the arm.

The wedding march was playing, and he turned away from the sight of Atalee drifting up the aisle on her own father's arm to meet her undeserving groom.

"Did you talk to her?" his father asked quietly.

He nodded. "Didn't do any good."

Tossing one last look up the long aisle, he found Atalee looking back at him before she turned to Johnny and joined hands with him.

Shaw walked out. Then he went straight to the Texas Rangers' office and put in for a transfer, which he got three weeks later.

GET WITHIN RANGE NOW

EM PETROVA
WWW.EMPETROVA.COM

Made in the USA
Monee, IL
04 September 2024

65141330R00138